The Pleasure Marriage

A Novel

Tahar Ben Jelloun

Translated from the French by Rita S. Nezami

CURBSTONE BOOKS/NORTHWESTERN UNIVERSITY PRESS
EVANSTON, ILLINOIS

Curbstone Books
Northwestern University Press
www.nupress.northwestern.edu

This is a work of fiction. Characters, places, and events are the product of the
author's imagination or are used fictitiously and do not represent actual people, places,
or events.

Printed in the United States of America

10   9   8   7   6   5   4   3   2   1

Library of Congress Cataloging-in-Publication Data

Names: Ben Jelloun, Tahar, 1944– author. | Nezami, Rita S., translator.
Title: The pleasure marriage : a novel / Tahar Ben Jelloun ; translated from the French
    by Rita S. Nezami.
Other titles: Mariage de plaisir. English
Description: Evanston, Illinois : Curbstone Books/Northwestern University Press,
    2021. | Originally published in French as Le Mariage de plaisir, by Éditions
    Gallimard, 2016.
Identifiers: LCCN 2021000527 | ISBN 9780810143593 (paperback)
Subjects: LCSH: Jealousy—Fiction. | Marriage (Islamic law)—Fiction. | Polygamy—
    Fiction. | Racism—Fiction. | Twins—Fiction. | Fès (Morocco)—Fiction.
Classification: LCC PQ3989.2.J4 M3713 2021 | DDC 843.914—dc23
LC record available at https://lccn.loc.gov/2021000527

For Amine

"O my sister, relate to us a story to beguile the waking hour of our night.

—Most willingly, answered Sheherazade, if this virtuous King permit me."

The King hearing these words, and being restless, was pleased with the idea of listening to the story; and thus, on the first night of the thousand and one, Sheherazade commenced her recitations.

"It has been related to me, O happy King, said Sheherazade, that there was once . . ."

THE THOUSAND AND ONE NIGHTS, TRANS. EDWARD WILLIAM LANE

The Pleasure Marriage

CONTENTS

A man can be honest in any sort of skin.

—HERMAN MELVILLE, *MOBY-DICK; OR, THE WHALE*

I came to poetry through the urgent need to denounce injustice, exploitation, humiliation. I know that's not enough to change the world. But to remain silent would be intolerable.

—TAHAR BEN JELLOUN

In *Le Mariage de plaisir*, Moroccan-born French writer Tahar Ben Jelloun explores a pleasure marriage and what follows after the union. The Arabic term for "pleasure marriage" is *nikah mut'ah*. It is also often called a "temporary marriage." This ancient Islamic practice historically enabled a man to have a legal wife for a short time in another country while traveling long distances for trade or other purposes.

Even though such a marriage is not intended to lead to a long-term relationship of love and respect, that is where this particular "pleasure marriage" leads. The temporary union of Nabou and Amir entails great pain and subjects them to fierce expressions of racism when they decide to have a traditional marriage, or *nikah*, in Morocco. Racism emerges because the woman is Senegalese and Black and her husband is from Fez, where fair skin is common.

Reading this intriguing novel in 2017, I immediately wanted to translate it because the protagonists' voices spoke to me deeply, and the themes of racism and illegal immigration are urgent and timely for the global community of English readers. Ben Jelloun's works are especially powerful because he lends his voice to the marginal and to those who have been silenced by the state and society. Readers cannot but relate to the characters' difficult conditions and struggles, which Ben Jelloun writes about with such immediacy that they could be his own. It is Ben Jelloun's moral imagination that gives him access to the minds of men and women and enables him to vividly represent their joys and sufferings. In a world plagued by racism and injustice, I felt it was a moral obligation to help make the novel accessible beyond the Francophone world.

Ben Jelloun uses a poetic French for the first five chapters of *Le Mariage de plaisir*. The language then changes from lyrical to simple, dry, and straightforward in the last three chapters as the themes become darker—brutal racism, blatant discrimination, illegal immigration, deportation-related violence, and death. These chapters may surprise readers as they seem as if they could be taken from another work. This mélange of poetry and harsh reality, of magic and global crisis, of fiction and nonfiction, gives rise to a story that has all the texture of complex reality.

While my interest has long been riveted by Ben Jelloun's focus on issues at the forefront of the global political conversation, I am equally intrigued by Ben Jelloun's lyrical French, infused with Arabic words and expressions and Moroccan cultural sensibilities. I strive to capture this Arabization in English by retaining Arabic words and cultural concepts. These words are infused with cultural and historical significance and many appear over and over in his works.

Some commonly used Arabic words (italicized in the text unless they can be found in *Webster's* dictionary) are: *adoul* (notary, marriage registrar, religious official), Ashura (a Muslim religious festival), *haram* (forbidden by Islamic law), Sunna (a body of established Islamic customs and beliefs), sura (a chapter or section of the Koran), djellaba (a widely worn long, loose garment), *taguia* (a small cap that resembles a kippah), hammam (like the Turkish bath in Morocco), medina (the old Arab quarter in North African towns), *kissaria* (a cluster of shops under a common roof), *ras el-hanout* (Moroccan spices), tagine (a Maghrebi dish), galette (buckwheat pancake), *tolbas* (Moroccan musicians), and many more. Because I lived in Morocco for several years, these words conjure visual images and personal experiences for me, and I feel transported to the heart of the culture and country.

Translating this novel also transported me to Senegal. Social, cultural, and religious ties between Morocco and Senegal date back centuries through trade and the spread of Islam, the predominant religion in both countries. The muezzins call Muslims to prayer from minarets in both Morocco and Senegal. When I think about the Senegal I know, I see the majestic baobab trees, the deep-blue Atlantic, and Ile Gorée, a tiny Senegalese island off the coast of Dakar known for its role in the Atlantic slave trade. I was transported to Ile Gorée the moment I encountered it in the novel and could imagine the untold numbers of slaves who were packed onto ships at the island beginning in 1536, when the Portuguese launched the slave trade, to the time the French halted it 312 years later. Though Senegalese women brought to Morocco by tradesmen were not named as slaves, these women were often treated as such in Moroccan society. So, when Nabou, the Senegalese wife of Ben Jelloun's male protagonist, Amir, arrives in Morocco, his first wife has no right to protest. It is a poignant commentary on the condition of women in 1950s Morocco that she sees no other way to express her anger than to attempt to harm Nabou. A result is that Nabou becomes yet another voiceless woman upon whom is visited racism and humiliation, a fate that also awaits her black son and grandson.

It is important to consider the nuances of the Arabic and other words that refer to black skin color. Along with the many frequently used Arabic words in the novel, some words used by Ben Jelloun required research. Some of these words that reflect the novel's historical and cultural context include: Nègre (Negro), Kahlouch (Black), *abid* (slave), *azzi* (someone with very dark skin), and "Jewess" (an archaic, and now offensive, word for a Jewish woman), along with "nigger" and "negress"—intensely pejorative and offensive words still used in Morocco. About these words, Ben Jelloun commented, "The words used to designate Blacks are obviously racist; some still use them, but it can be said that there is some progress against anti-black racism." The way the word "Jewess" is used in the culture is especially difficult to capture. "It depends if the word is accompanied with a grimace," Ben Jelloun wrote. "Then it becomes insulting." Morocco is not immune from the ugliness of antisemitism, although Ben Jelloun suggests that, when it occurs, it should not be confused with the virulence of European antisemitism. There is no question, Ben Jelloun said, "that fanatical Islamists are frankly antisemites."

There are some moments in the text that deserve special mention. There is confusion about the date that Fez was founded. In the French edition, Ben Jelloun cites 808; here, with his permission, we have changed that to 789. Historical sources document that Idriss I founded Fez on the east bank of the Fez River in 789; his son, Idriss II, built a settlement on the west bank in 808. Queried about this, Ben Jelloun wrote that, "Yes, Fez was founded in 789, but became a livable city only in 808." This is a novel dense with history and culture, and many references required investigation. I have tried to render the most accurate text possible in light of the best information currently available.

I have translated Tahar Ben Jelloun for more than fifteen years. I first became interested in the author and began translating his work in 2003, when his autobiographical novel *L'Ecrivain public* (1983) captured my interest. By translating this work, *The Public Scribe*, three chapters of which were published in English in different literary journals, I got to know more about the writer, his life, and his values, as well as to appreciate his poetic French and to admire his keen interest in modern society and the human condition.

Over the years, as I continued reading both Ben Jelloun's nonfiction and fiction and translating various short stories and a book on the Arab Spring for publication (*By Fire: Writings on the Arab Spring*, Northwestern University Press, 2016), I identified his exploration of universal themes that resonated with my own interests: injustice, corruption, exploitation, unemployment, racial and gender discrimination, illegal immigration, dictatorship, masculinity and femininity.

My work has benefited immeasurably from Monsieur Ben Jelloun's generosity during the translation process. We met first in 2005. Even though he lives and writes in Paris, Tangier also offers him the perfect place to work quietly amid the culture he represents and interrogates. I have remained close to the Moroccan culture, the people, and the cultural sensibilities since my years there. I owe my capacity to faithfully translate the Moroccan way of being to my continuous engagement with the country and its people.

Translation for me is a visual and deeply personal experience. While I was translating *L'Ecrivain public* I struggled to understand some of Ben Jelloun's references. It was only on a return trip to Tangier that the phrase "Le mur des parreseux" ("the idler's wall") gave up its secret: As I walked one day toward the main square at the end of Tangier's Boulevard Pasteur, I noticed a low stone wall overlooking the Mediterranean. Upon the wall sat young men gazing across the sea toward Spain, perhaps dreaming of crossing the Strait of Gibaltar. Here was what Ben Jelloun had in mind. In a single phrase, he captured Morocco's ongoing crisis of chronic unemployment and the huge population of jobless men who long to make the trip across the Mediterranean Sea to find their futures in Europe. This theme finds resonance in *The Pleasure Marriage*, in which one of the main characters has the same dream, to find the dignity of employment by immigrating to Spain.

Another day, walking toward the bustling medina, I finally understood the meaning of another word Ben Jelloun used in both novels—"*kissaria*," which might be translated in American English as "shopping center," which is dreadfully wrong. Before me was a cluster of small stores facing each other inside a one-story building. My solution to this non-translatability problem was to leave "*kissaria*" in my translation and explain it in a glossary. I would have been guilty of domestication had I chosen "shopping center," and I am committed to avoiding linguistic domestication that strips from a text the essence of its cultural sensibility, which lies in the specific connotative associations that only a writer's original lexical choice can convey.

I will relate just one more delightful illustration from *L'Ecrivain public* of domestication-avoidance. Wrestling with how to handle for American readers Ben Jelloun's "mon petit foi"—words of endearment meaning "my little liver" that the writer's mother uses for her son—my default option was to simply drop in the wan English "my sweetheart." Instead, I left undisturbed the original French and offered a brief glossary explanation. I trust readers will gladly peek at the glossary as a small price to pay for experiencing the authentic Moroccan sensibility that *remains* authentic only by translating "mon petit foie" as "my little liver."

I see literary translation as creative writing that requires careful lexical research to find the greatest possible textual clarity that does not betray either the writer's intention or the culture's sensibilities. Translators become researchers because they are hypersensitive to recovering in the target language every cultural, social, historical, and political moment. The hard truth, though, is that, regardless of linguistic command and exhaustive research, translators inevitably encounter words and expressions that are simply untranslatable because many realities and experiences do not exist in the target language. Yet, there is immense joy when we find language that captures as much as possible of the original meaning. That doesn't always happen, though; there will be semantic slippage. When that occurs, it is the glossary that allows otherwise tormented translators to sleep nights knowing that it will help close the gap between the writer's language and the lines that eventually find their way into readers' hands.

TRANSLATOR'S ACKNOWLEDGMENTS

This translation is dedicated to my parents. I would like to express my admiration and gratitude to my publisher father, the late Ruhul Amin Nezami, for inspiring me to read world literature and translate. I have continuously drawn strength from my mother, Akhtarun Nesa, whose courage and compassion have inspired me since childhood. And I would like to thank Jeffrey Green for his edits to my translation and suggestions about my preface.

The Pleasure Marriage

Chapter 1

There was once in the city of Fez a storyteller who resembled no other. His name was Goha. He had dark brown skin, a dry and hard body, a penetrating look, and a great sense of precision. He arrived from the South after the heavy rains, usually at the beginning of spring, settled himself on a square at the entrance of the old city, sometimes in Batha, sometimes in Bab Boujloud, placed his belongings on the ground, and waited for a circle to form around him. Coming from a great culture as much Arab as Berber, he had the gift of an astonishing imagination; he was known for his severity of judgment, and also for the rigidity of his ideas. He had his followers as well as his critics, who waited the entire year for his arrival and never missed any of his stories. They passed the news around: "He has arrived!" They closed their stores and went to listen to him. He didn't just tell them stories. He also loved to bring up historical circumstances to make them think. He never approached problems directly; he liked to go around them. He was, they said, a master of this technique that consisted of looking at the present while keeping a foot in the past, which is often less glorious than one thinks. He didn't hide his anger toward the way Morocco allowed herself to be taken over by France during the protectorate. He said with irony: "This is how we gave in to Lalla La France, the great country of Light and intelligence, who has become bloated by her grotesque appetite. Algeria wasn't enough, nor was Tunisia; she had to also swallow our country! Poor Morocco! Poor Lalla França!" Suddenly, in the middle of his storytelling, he stopped, drank a sip of water, grabbed a broom, and started sweeping the square. When he departed, the storyteller always left behind his bowl filled with coins, preferring to leave it for the beggars, who, he said, needed it more than he did. The police sent someone to listen to his stories many times. But nobody ever found anything with which to reproach him; he told stories and didn't cause any disturbance. During his storytelling, he played all kinds of roles at the same time; he sometimes disguised himself, assumed provocative poses, and, especially, knew how to retain his audience's full attention at all times. He was an actor as well as a poet who, to intrigue his listeners, always loved to begin with the words:

"You who are going to lend your ears to my stories, listen to the advice of someone who grew up in the desert, and who was always very passionate: be mean! Don't hesitate: be wicked! If I get out of line, call me back to order; your meanness should always remain awake. And especially don't lower your guard, sympathize with the Evil, this Evil that grows within us as a poisonous plant, as a stinking and killer seaweed that feeds our bile and turns it into a poison that is poured into the furrows of life. Be mean. I don't want your mercy. My age, my fractures, my many flaws, my memory that comes and goes, which can betray me at any moment and get my stories mixed up, confused, and will mislead you. Be mean, and you'll live a long time! Cruel and bad. Ruthless and without qualms. Be mean, and you'll save time!"

The storyteller was wise. He knew it was useless to ask people to be good, and that kindness did not need crutches to move forward. One evening when he was in Fez, while a small circle started to gather around him, Goha decided to change his story and started telling a tale that no one had ever heard before:

"Just this once, I'm going to tell you a love story. This doesn't happen all the time, and I'm not going to make it a custom. But this evening, I will tell you of a mad and impossible love experienced until the characters' last breaths. As you'll see, behind this miraculous story there is also a lot of hatred and contempt, meanness and cruelty. It's normal. That's how people are. I would want you to remember this so that you're not astonished by anything."

* * *

There was once in the city of Fez a little boy named Amir, born into a family of traders who were said to be descendants of the Prophet.

It was the day of the first rains. His younger brother had just turned one, when, suddenly, word spread in the town that the Beggar had come back. Those who knew him said that his voice, deep and strong, was terrifying; that his eyelids always trembled slightly, nervously; that all it took was a gesture of his hand to convince anyone to stay away from crossing his path. Everybody agreed that he had an unbearable odor, which preceded him and remained long after his departure. No one has dared until now to approach him and offer alms. His face, however, was a different matter. His eyes, large and clear, gave off a strange light.

What did the Beggar want? Where did he come from? What was his name? Nobody knew. But children named him El Ghool (the monster), El Ghaddar (the traitor), or El Henche (the serpent). Grownups called him Ould Lehrâme (the bastard), the one who predicts misfortune.

A few days after the Beggar's visit, a typhus epidemic spread in Fez. Amir's little brother died within a few hours. Amir and his parents were lucky to escape the disease.

After a few anxious days, Fez was mostly out of danger. The epidemic moved itself to the mountains and villages, where death had so many people to take away. Fez acquired the status of "Sacred City" overnight, without any interference by religious authority.

But secretly, Fez feared the return of the Beggar, whose visit remained in people's memories. Luckily, until then, prayers at the Grande Mosquée seemed to have kept him away.

Throughout his childhood, from the first rains of the season, the sound of the Beggar's deep voice resonated in Amir's ears, and an unimaginable fear seized him. As he grew older, Amir managed to forget him, and he persuaded himself, on the other hand, that if death had passed by him, it was so that he may accomplish some great purpose in the world.

Reaching adult age, Amir became a handsome man, fair skinned, of medium height, a little plump, with fine lips and a well-drawn mouth, and slightly drooping shoulders. Like his parents, he became a trader in the old town of Fez, in the Diwane neighborhood. He was a good man, optimistic and without imagination, who hardly missed any of the five daily prayers. He was married very young to Lalla Fatma—an arranged marriage with a young woman from a good family of Fez—and he was the father of four children. Three sons and a daughter.

During that time, Fez was far removed from the world. It had been more than forty years since Morocco was made a French protectorate, and the old Fassi aristocracy that controlled the city had maintained its authority with remarkable calm and serenity. They were not concerned about what was happening outside the medina*. For them, the world ended here, in the medina's alleys, in its old houses, some of which were palaces, all waiting for the eternal return of the lemon season. The artisans made handicrafts, the traders traded, and the lords rode on horseback in the narrow streets and had no doubt about their class superiority. They were the ones, by the way, who in the nineteenth century had chosen the small square between Achabine and Chémayine, deep in the medina, to set up on Thursday every month a market, where black slaves brought from Africa were sold.

Slavery was common. It was seen everywhere, and the Fassis had no wish to change anything at all about the injustice of the world. They were satisfied living according to traditions and felt they had the obligation to perpetuate and protect them. The first slaves arrived in Morocco because of trade that the most enterprising Fassis had with the nearest African countries. Even though they shared the same continent, the Fassis were far from considering themselves Africans. The Fassis were fair skinned, thus they felt superior to the Blacks no matter where they came from.

In Fez, on the eve of the country's independence, nothing was to change, nothing could change. The French watched this from a distance. A cover of wool and cotton lay over the city. So many stories and secrets had been kept there over the centuries. Strangely, no one was there to tell them, to reveal them, to expel them from this society that was satisfied with itself, its origins, its traditions, its culture, which they confused with the values of Islam. Many Jews and Muslims who were chased out of Andalusia by Isabella the Catholic had nevertheless found refuge in Fez and had contributed to the wealth of the city, its renewal, and its originality. One could, it seems, be converted there without even changing one's name. But this time was in the distant past.

To have a supply of spices and other rare products, once a year Amir left Fez to go to Senegal for many months. His father and grandfather, who traded there before him, used to take a wife for the duration of their stay. Amir, who liked to respect the rules, and who would blame himself if he were to do something that was forbidden by religion, had consulted about this practice with Moulay Ahmad, an important professor of theology at the Université Al Quaraouiyine*, and had asked him if "the pleasure marriage," as it was called, wasn't a sin, an act that would go against his faith and offend his wife. In truth, Amir had some doubts about this practice.

Moulay Ahmad reassured him. He quoted from verse 24 of the sura* "The Wives": " 'It is permissible for you to use your right to marry honestly and not to live in concubinage without being married. It is an obligation for you to offer an agreed-upon dowry to the one with whom you will have consummated the marriage.' In other words, it's legal for a man who is away from home for long periods of time to contract a marriage of pleasure, enjoyment, well-being, which guarantees the wife a dowry and respect from the one who married her. God instituted this to fight against prostitution.

"It's true," said Moulay Ahmad, "that a pleasure marriage contracted out of the conjugal home for a given period has the sense of a forbidden perfume, which could excite the lower instincts of the man. It should not in any case, however, be understood as an encouragement to humiliate the legitimate woman left behind at home, or to mistreat the one with whom you contract a marriage for a certain period. This notion of pleasure is linked to the brevity of the relationship. The other marriage that took place earlier and for procreation does not leave out pleasure, but lessens it."

Amir listened to the professor very attentively:

"It is said that our beloved Prophet had contracted a pleasure marriage, but that the second caliph prohibited this practice before he died. In fact, it is one of the points of discrepancy between the Shiites, who authorize it, and the Sunnis, who have doubts about it. But many discussions on this subject had taken place among Sunni theologians, and al-Châfi, for example, validated such a marriage as long as the intentions of the couple are clear and the duration is limited in time. That is why this practice has survived until today, the essential thing being to remain within the limits of having decency and respect for the wife."

Amir, feeling reassured and appeased, contracted, during each of his journeys in Africa, a marriage of pleasure to protect himself from sin.

After spending a year trading in Fez and taking care of his family, it was time for Amir to return to Africa again. He decided to go this year with Karim, his youngest son. All preparations were made for traveling, and when evening came, Amir had trouble falling asleep. He let his thoughts wander and join the rumors of the city of Fez, which was plunged into the night's darkness. There he came across the troubled souls of the sleepers, and the silhouettes of those women who, at night, know how to move their bodies and their shapes so well that they disturb the traders' dreams and give them such extraordinary colors that they can make any man fantasize in the folds of the night . . .

The day before his departure, being disturbed more than ever before by these visions, Amir got up and went to the garden of his house. He walked around for a moment in the dim light and discovered, among the bottle-green branches of a palm tree, a white flower in bloom, solitary and proud, which seemed to announce the arrival of summer, and, later, the dates of autumn.

Amir observed this miracle of nature, and he thanked God for having allowed such beauty to adorn his garden. For a long time he observed this flower that had a brilliant whiteness and thought of the young Peul* whom he had met during his last travels, and whom he hoped to find soon, far from this garden, in another country, another world, another time. And he said to himself that this flower resembles her so much. It is as white as this young woman, perfumed with amber and sandalwood, is black.

Chapter 2

When Karim left with his father for Senegal, he had just turned thirteen and wore with pride the fourth medal he won at the last swimming competition where he had excelled. During their stay in Senegal, his father wanted him to spend a few days with a wise, old Senegalese from Gorée Island who was reputed to treat children born with a handicap.

Karim wasn't a child like any other. He was lively and intelligent, but he had a disability. At that time, such children were somewhat left on their own; they were allowed to go out alone, then to return, and if they got lost, there was always someone to bring them home.

At Karim's birth, Touria, the midwife, declared that this child had a pure heart, white as silk, and that it was necessary to let him live and develop in his own rhythm. His mother, Lalla Fatma, cried, while his father, Amir, tried to accept the midwife's words. He sent for a French doctor to examine Karim. But during the consultation, Amir didn't quite understand what the specialist was saying. He heard complex words like "chromosome," "trisomy," "Down syndrome." The doctor grabbed a piece of paper and made a drawing of a tree branch with lines on both sides, explaining to him that there was something unwanted that his son carried in him that would delay his development, but that it was not serious, for these children had a very short life expectancy, and that soon he would die and so the family would be rid of him . . . The Frenchman was acting in good faith, repeating what he had been taught, and didn't seem to be aware that he was badly hurting a father. Before leaving, he leaned toward Amir and whispered: "You know, even General De Gaulle had a child like yours, yet . . . Very few people knew about it, but they whispered in the army that it was for him the only defeat in his life! The day his daughter died, he might have said: 'Now, she is like all others.'"

Amir thanked the Frenchman, paid for the consultation, and went to see to his wife, who couldn't stop crying. The wet nurse, who was present during the consultation, tried to console them both. Understanding that only Amir was in a state to listen, she tried to comfort him:

"This child is good luck, it is a sign from God, a good fortune that God has offered to you. These are children who have this peculiarity of not knowing anything evil at all and are incapable of leaving the path of goodness. We should love them, as they have an infinite amount of affection. We should not reject or hide them. I know some who have continued to live as adults, and many people visit them, as though they are saints or angels. This child is a light, you will see, he will lighten up your life."

As a good believer, Amir accepted this fate and said to himself: If God allowed this child to be born, it is because he has his reasons. Who am I to challenge the divine will? This child is a blessing; he will live his life, and I will be by his side until my last breath. God is great. I know what our Prophet said: "The believer is often tested by God to know if he is capable of enduring a misfortune."

Lalla Fatma stopped speaking, stared at the ceiling, and from that moment refused to breastfeed the infant. For the first time since their marriage, Amir spoke to her in a harsh tone. She had to accept the reality. The harsh words that he spoke first shook her up and then made her cry even more. Then, after a moment of silence, she stretched out her arms to take her baby and gave him her breast.

Since then, Karim had a special place in the family. He grew up loved and pampered. Every time a new doctor came to Fez, Amir consulted him to find out if his son's condition would get better one day. But he understood well that this child needed just one thing: love. Feeling loved, that's what made him normal and happy.

When Karim turned twelve, his father made him a promise: "The next time I travel to Senegal, I'll take you with me!"

Mad with joy, Karim rushed to the out-of-tune old piano, and played an air to express his happiness. His brothers and sisters didn't have any say in this. They couldn't oppose their father's decisions. That was the traditional way. Children didn't raise their voices when they spoke to their parents, they kissed their parents' hands and shoulders, and they lowered their eyes when they spoke. This is how it used to be.

A few months later, at the beginning of winter, Amir asked his wife to pack his and Karim's luggage. They left the house in the middle of the night, crossing deserted Fez, which made their departure seem magical, unreal.

The journey by train, carriage, and camelback lasted more than two weeks. The weather was mild and the stops fairly frequent. After the last evening prayer, Amir used this moment to tell his son what he had learned about this continent and its people. He said: "I know I don't need to tell you; you are kind and intelligent. In this country, you must above all show respect! If you wish to be treated well and respected, begin by behaving in an irreproachable manner. Let respect and generosity guide your actions.

The people there are very sensitive and will give you a hundredfold of what you offer them. They have been so humiliated and scorned by the colonialists, by all the Whites who came from France and Belgium, that they are suspicious of all white-skinned people. But don't forget that we too are Africans. We are not black, but we belong to this continent and to these peoples. So remember that our beloved Prophet freed Bilal Ibn Rabah, the black slave who had a beautiful voice. He had been appointed by Muhammad as the first muezzin* of Islam. Unfortunately, slavery is still a tradition for those who feel superior. You'll see, we'll be received with a lot of friendship. So let us be worthy of this welcome and this hospitality!" Then, as if to bring some balance, he added: "But don't think that everyone is as good as you; the wicked exist everywhere, so be careful when I am not with you."

Karim listened to Amir religiously. His father's blessings were important to him. It was out of the question to disagree with him or challenge his words. Amir said, somewhat to justify himself: "The Koran advises us to have absolute respect for the father and the mother, as well as for those who share their knowledge with us, teachers, philosophers, scholars, or the simple schoolteacher." He added: "Success is impossible without this blessing; that's how it is, respect is a mark of humility, the best way to learn and move forward." Karim understood perfectly everything his father said to him. Even though he had remarkable insight, it was difficult for him to speak or develop his thoughts. Sometimes he got irritated and became red because the words did not come out, or they came out in distorted, small pieces. He repeated the same sound, stuttered, as if begging some inner force to help him speak. Amir, from the beginning, had decided to treat him as a child who had no problems while realizing that his disability existed and that it had to be taken into account in certain situations. Despite Amir's wishes, Lalla Fatma had trouble with this child and preferred to take care of the other three. But Karim was very loving toward his mother. Each time he told her with his awkward words how much he loved her, she cried. Instead of rejoicing, she turned her head, looking for a handkerchief to wipe away her tears. One day, he said to her: "I too, I ... I ... cry ..."

The caravan man was a Sahrawi who spoke very little. His skin tanned by the sun, his body dry, he moved forward, sure of himself. He wore an old rifle on a shoulder strap and a dagger around his waist. This was during the time when highway bandits attacked travelers. The man knew the paths to avoid and guided his clients safely. For him, the desert had no secrets. Because of this, the journey lasted one or two days longer. Neither Karim nor his father was in a hurry, and above all, they didn't question the guide, who was also a good cook. He knew that the Fassis were delicate people, accustomed to fine cuisine, neither too spicy nor too greasy. He made them crepes filled with pieces of preserved meat and hard-boiled eggs with cumin. The meals ended with some dates. Sometimes he gave them camel milk, but he noticed that they had to force themselves to swallow it. They preferred green tea with mint leaves. He put too much sugar, so every time Amir and his son had to ask for hot water to dilute the sugar a little. This made him laugh.

The Sahrawi was a former warrior. He fought against the Spanish army, which in 1934 had settled in the southern provinces of Morocco, including Sidi Ifni, his native city. The country was under the French protectorate, part of which was occupied by Spain and led by a general named Franco.

One evening, the caravan man told them about what this anti-colonial war was like: "The Spanish had no shame; they behaved like thugs and saw us as beasts. They were soldiers without any class; they despised us, and it was said that they had been punished and sent into the desert, about which they knew nothing. They drank alcohol and behaved without any respect for our families. One day, a father whose daughter had been kidnapped by a group of drunken soldiers seized a large knife and planted it in the neck of a low-level officer. The man was executed at once. His funeral the following day was an opportunity for us to express our anger. The army fired at us. Three people died and five were wounded. From that moment, the resistance was organized spontaneously. The army understood that we didn't accept this occupation. We were few and quiet; we sabotaged what the soldiers tried to build. Hatred was deep on both sides except that we, *we* were on the side of law and justice. Why did these wretched soldiers come to occupy our land? We gave them a hard time. One day they will definitely leave, and I hope they will never set foot in our country again."

One night, as they were about to sleep, Karim jumped up and shouted:

"Lion! I . . . I saw a lion . . ."

The Sahrawi said seriously:

"There are no lions here."

Karim kept insisting, and the guide turned his back to him. Karim's father felt worried, knowing that his son never said anything randomly or to joke. He asked the man to go and check, which he did reluctantly. A few minutes later, the guide returned and appeared frightened, saying that there was indeed a lion, but now it was gone. He started getting his old gun ready:

"From now on, I will believe everything that Karim tells me!"

Sleep was short and especially agitated. They set out again in the middle of the night, tired and silent. At one moment, Amir asked his son if he saw anything dangerous, or heard strange noises. Karim, half-asleep, responded:

"No, no, nothing . . . Just a piano . . . I can see, I . . . can hear it . . . girl pi . . . piano . . ."

Karim played the piano without having taken lessons. He tapped on the piano and it wasn't bad; it was a gift. During the journey through the desert, certain melodies came back to his soul. He missed music.

The Sahrawi was surprised:

"First the lion and now the piano!"

Karim pointed his finger to his forehead and said:

"It's inside!"

"You can hear music?"

"Yes, go . . . good mu . . . sic . . ."

"You are lucky."

Karim thus listened to a concerto from memory. He seemed completely into it. Suddenly, he stopped and said:

"The pi . . . piano needs to pee!"

He moved away from the caravan and peed while laughing.

Early one morning they arrived in Ndar, also called Saint-Louis, the first city to be founded by Europeans in West Africa. The sky was white and the air humid. This made Karim say: "It's as if we are in a hammam*." Amir explained to him the difference between the two countries' climates. He had become a connoisseur of African civilization. He said: "We are now approaching Dakar, the capital. We are at the mouth of the Senegal River. Look at this vegetation and these wonders created by water. They are water trees that don't bear fruit; they are just trees that grow on the riverbank to give travelers shade." The caravan man was so happy to have brought them to this point that he suddenly became very talkative. He spoke nonstop about the beauty of this country, about the people's kindness, and especially about the availability of its women. Like a guide, he told them the history of this city, emphasizing the prosperity of its gold and ivory trade. Amir intervened to remind him that this was also the city where slaves were bought. The guide added that it was from here that a French pilot had taken off in a small plane to go very far! Karim, being interested in the story, asked where the man was now, and what he had managed to do. His father promised to find out. For the moment, they decided to put down their luggage and wash up. Not far from where they were, there was a small lake where children were bathing and making a lot of noise. Amir made his ablutions, looked for the direction of Mecca, and prayed to thank God for having permitted him and his son to arrive in good health at this magical place with its old, colonial buildings. During the night, the caravan man woke up Karim and said: "Mermoz, that's the pilot, his name was Mermoz, I remember now. He went all the way to Merica, Americ . . ."

They spent two days and nights in Ndar, and, early in the morning, they took the road to Dakar. The journey lasted a day and part of a night. Amir wanted to wait until sunrise to enter Dakar, a city that reminded him of Casablanca with its well-planned avenues and modern buildings. The caravan man was all excited. Amir paid him and said: "Try to find us again in two months. We won't be far from Moh's."

Moh was the owner of L'Ami des Voyageurs, a small hotel where Amir liked to stay before "officially" going to the center of Dakar. They washed up, ate, and rested a little. They were received like princes. Then, Amir went out, telling Karim: "Don't wait up for me; eat while I'm gone. Moh will take very good care of you."

Karim went out for a walk. Amir didn't have to tell him to be careful. He knew that his son had a particularly good sense of direction and that he would always get back without any problem. While walking around, Karim had a strange but pleasant feeling: he felt secure here, as though all the Senegalese people were family members. However, he had trouble getting used to this thick heat and the harsh sun. He was hot, sweating. He returned to the hotel and put on a large and light *gandoura**. His European clothes were not suitable for this climate.

Not long ago, during his travel to Senegal, Amir got into the habit of signing a pleasure marriage contract with Nabou, a superb, one-meter-eighty-tall Peul woman. He returned every year at the same time, left his things at Moh's, renewed his marriage contract with Nabou, settled into the house that he built for her, and lived with her as a loved and satisfied master. Luckily, they didn't have children. For Amir, Nabou was a magician, a little bit of a witch, and especially very beautiful and sensual.

The young woman had stopped going to the French school after receiving her *brevet**. She was proud and was seen by her family as someone "who knew how to deal with foreigners." She often worked as a public scribe: she edited love letters for women abandoned by soldiers, and she also wrote complaints sent to the colonial administration.

In her arms, Karim's father lost his head. She reserved for him sexual acrobatics that fulfilled him and emptied him of his energy. Each time he said his daily prayers, he raised his joined hands to the sky to thank God for letting him know this woman who gave him the kind of pleasure that he had never before known or found with any other woman. But there weren't only these moments of pleasure; sometimes Amir allowed himself a little romanticism learned from Arab and Persian poets. He passionately recited poems. It made her laugh. She never said anything, allowing herself to be loved, and did everything for the happiness of her husband. They were happy, and Amir couldn't understand why relationships in Fez were so complicated.

One year, he wanted to take her to Mecca for pilgrimage. But he discovered that she wasn't Muslim, that her religion had nothing to do with monotheism, and that deep down she wasn't religious at all. When she felt like praying, she went to spend the night under the oldest tree, the biggest and the most beautiful at the edge of the city. It was a majestic tree that no construction company dared cut down. Even the French who had carried out the work were obliged to go around it to construct roads. Nabou caressed its bark, talked to it, and felt good because she was convinced that the ancestors had left a part of their soul there. This tree was her God, her refuge, her sacred object. She called it "Hadji Baba." Its shade soothed her, its presence and old age comforted her. She liked confiding in it in solitude at the moment when the sun went down, leaving the air like a great basin drenched in gray, blue, and silver powder. For her, this was the moment to place her cheek against one of the branches and talk to the tree in Wolof, her mother tongue: "These days my thoughts have been abandoned by light; there's a darkness that I don't like. Perhaps I've made some errors, mistakes, or simple blunders. Yesterday, by mistake I walked on a piece of bread. I picked it up, kissed it, and then gave it to the chicken, but I wasn't happy with myself. The other day, a strange feeling made me tear up though I had no reason to cry. The feeling came along with a piercing music that reminded me of the unpleasant sound made by knife-sharpening men in the streets. I saw a long caravan descend from the mountain, preceded by an immense yellow flag that fluttered in the strong wind. Some men without arms, others without legs, gathered at the city's entrance. I saw myself as a child, running like a gazelle, my skin and eyes full of sand. It was a time when everything was possible. The other morning I saw some women with sad faces on the verge of crying. Nobody knew why. I looked at the sky and didn't see anything reassuring. In the past, the blue made me want to dance. For a while, now, the blue has disappeared, and here I am on my knees before you, O Hadji Baba. Have I misunderstood your messages, your words that the wind brings to me? Have I lost all faith in my soul?

"My grandmother shared a revelation. She said that I'm made like dreams, and that my eyes are already elsewhere; she also told me that dreams are nothing other than messages that death sends us so that we may get used to its existence. Despite everything, the hope of finding my white man, the one who visits me once a year, shakes me up. He's a good man. Give him the strength to make me happy . . . He knows, he can guess that I'm not a faithful wife; how can one be when she's born with a desire that's stronger than her senses? It's not a bad thing, we don't talk about it, and he knows it but doesn't say anything. The truth is, I don't know anything.

"In the winter, it's my cousin Wad who keeps me warm when I'm cold. He knows my body perfectly and its needs. He knows how to give it life and energy. We don't talk about it. All it takes is for our eyes to meet; I get up and he follows me. I know what he's going to give me and what I'm going to offer him. I love these moments, just before going to bed. I dream, and I feel joy in my heart and in my body. At times I tremble from pleasure.

"In the spring, it's Degaule, our neighbor who could have been my father's age, who invites himself to my place and caresses me the entire night without doing anything else. I let him—I admit it pleases me, relaxes me. I'm between his hands and his mouth, and sometimes I doze off to his tender caresses. He's an expert. The following day I receive from him baskets full of fruit and vegetables, pieces of fabric and incense, and sometimes dry meat. Enough to eat for over a month. As soon as he senses that my provisions are finished, he comes knocking on my window.

"I also give in to the advances made by the young French doctor who says he's madly in love with me; it makes me laugh. When he comes, his entire body sweats and becomes red. This scares me. He tells me it's because of his shyness and feeling of guilt. One day I asked him to explain what guilt means. He told me that he's married to a white woman who was waiting for him in Dijon, and that when he comes to see me, he feels as though someone is punching him in the chest; he feels pain, and then, the same person starts blaming him; he has tried blocking his ears, but he hears the shouting, so he lowers his head and asks Camille, who's back in Dijon, to forgive him. This is what guilt means. Me, I don't know such punching or shouting. I give him pleasure; he gives me a lot of medicine that I distribute among friends and family. The other day he offered me a perfume from Paris. Since that time, I've been wearing it, and I feel as though I'm a seller of sex. It smells strange; I prefer natural amber and musk; I prefer the black soap and *rassoul** that Amir brings me from Fez.

"Ah, my master, my man, the only prince who renders me truly beautiful. When Amir is here, I'm totally his; no one dares to approach me. I fly the Moroccan flag on the roof, and I burn incense of paradise. Everyone knows my man has arrived. Neighbors drop in to wish me happiness and prosperity, and even if they are jealous, they don't hurt me. I prepare myself over two days to welcome him with my body and soul. I change my behavior. I mean, I feel as though I have become another woman; I belong to him and I like this sensation of being his, entirely his. Perhaps this situation can't last forever, and it may not be moral. Today I find myself at your feet, clutching your roots, O Hadji Baba. I am weak, and I place myself at your mercy! Each time Amir visits me, he takes me to the scribes at the mosque, and they write up a temporary contract. I think it's called the 'marriage of pleasure.' Amir wants to be in good standing with his religion. I have nothing to complain about; he spoils me, and I take very good care of him.

"One day, I asked him: 'Why is our marriage called a marriage of pleasure? What kind of marriage is the other, the one with your wife in Morocco?' He looked at me and said: 'There, it's tradition; here, it's freedom!'

"My mother is mean to me. She needs money, and I give her some when I can, but she tells me: 'It's dirty money.' I don't know how to calm her. She could never tolerate the fact that I escaped from her and that men fall into my arms . . . I don't do anything bad!"

This year Nabou was anxious. On top of the mounting and violent jealousy among her neighbors, the spirits had convinced her that on account of her infidelity to Amir, she was going to die under unexpected circumstances. Would she be thrown from the top of a cliff, bitten by a viper with a human face, crushed by a mad elephant, hung to the bottom of a well, choked with a jute or plastic bag, or poisoned by the neighbor? Or would she simply become a victim of cardiac arrest during her sleep while she dreamed of her Arab prince? She persuaded herself that she would die by drowning. She looked around, but there was no lake or ocean, at least she couldn't see any from where she was. So she told herself that the spirits had been mistaken, that they had better leave her in peace and go elsewhere.

When she went to see her baobab tree one night, she felt nothing. It was silent, impassive, absent. With her fingers she broke a piece of bark and started to chew it. It was so bitter that she spat it out and ran off. Yet she went back, knelt down before the baobab, and asked for forgiveness. A branch leaned down and stroked her shoulders. This didn't comfort her. Panicking, she felt her fever rise. Was her last hour near? Yet she was still young and robust. Sweating a lot, she saw red stars in the sky, a sign that she was struck by a curse. Nothing was in its right place. She suddenly felt immensely alone, and pulling out of her pocket a small mirror, she looked at herself. What she saw terrified her. She saw a wicked face, old and wrinkled, her eyes were yellow, and there was drool at the corners of her lips. She turned her head toward her neighbor, a mother of eight children, without a husband, without support. Nabou knew that this woman was consumed by envy and jealousy. She had probably succeeded in casting a spell on her, especially since the famous Dia, the greatest sorcerer in the country, had just stayed in the city after working on a very rich man who had lost his sexual power. Dia had the reputation of melting iron just by staring at it. He knew how to heal tormented souls and get rid of the pain from bodies threatened by disease. He could also disturb one's soul and make sleep impossible. It was said that is why a chief had gone mad and had jumped off the top of a cliff.

For the first time, Nabou was scared, she who had never experienced this sensation. She discovered panic that turned everything upside down, poured mud into the clear water, pulled out the roots, and painted the world in gray and black. Fear gripped her; she felt her body shaken, agitated, mistreated. She said to herself: "I am like a cloth wrung by fate; what drips is not water but drops of blood, mine, which I must be losing because I am being punished even though I have not done anything bad, at least nothing really bad. The presage is insistent. What to do? Whom to turn to? I am alone and am struggling in a dark forest with vicious shadows whose goal is to make me go crazy. I promise to devote myself entirely and exclusively to my man, my one and only man, Sidi Amir, the most generous of all men."

A few days before Amir's arrival, Nabou had the idea of visiting Moha, the old sage in Thiès, a small town east of Dakar. Moha was the maddest and at the same time the most humane of the Tijane brotherhood. He maintained epistolary relations with the Sufis of Fez, who spent much of their time working on sacred texts. His words were known to appease and to restore hope and patience. He said everything he thought; he had nothing to lose, and even his life was of little importance to him. He lived inside an old baobab that had died a long time ago and had no power anymore. He had dug a hollow into the tree and lived in it alone. From time to time a stray dog found refuge there. He shared his meager meal with the dog and then let it go. Nabou couldn't go to see him empty-handed. She offered him a jar of honey and olives that Amir had brought her from Fez during his last visit.

Moha reminded her that her beauty could be the source of all her problems. Jealousy was like a spider that wove its web all around her soul. It was necessary to thwart this evil spell to allow her to live in peace. She confessed to him that she would very much like Amir to propose one day to take her with him to Fez. Moha grimaced. He knew this city and its people well:

"They are civilized people, but they feel superior to us, in any case they are persuaded that they were selected by God. They are good Muslims, good people, but they love to subjugate and dominate. You are black. I am métis*. We have no place in their hearts, in their city. But who knows? One can come across generous families, respectful toward humanity. If you must go, make sure you take something to protect yourself. I am not a sorcerer, but I have talismans in which with my own hands I have inserted verses from the Koran. If you believe in it, they will protect you. Otherwise, you will have to face difficult problems alone. If you want, I will send a letter to Si Mostafa, a man with whom I correspond and who is the imam at the Grande Mosquée and the university of the old city."

Nabou reminded him that she was not Muslim.

"It is time for you to embrace this religion, which, when accurately understood, can be of great help. People have always needed to calm their anxieties. I think they created religions to endure life and its mysteries, death being the main enigma that nobody has ever resolved. I believe all the prophets. I know some verses by heart, and I can say that Islam, Catholicism, and Judaism are religions that resemble each other. Their mission is to appease man and to warn him when he goes beyond his limits; this is why hell and paradise exist."

She asked him what needed to be done to become a Muslim. Moha advised her to speak to her husband. He was in the best position to guide her into the religion of Muhammad. Moha asked her to thank Amir, because the honey and olives from Fez were exceptional. She left calmly, having decided to become Muslim.

On the way back, she stopped in front of her baobab and stared at it fixedly as if she were asking for its permission, blessing, and support. She was in fact pleased with this initiative, which she thought was going to release her from her fears, from the evil eye that jealous women inflicted on her. She said, "Allah is great, I am no longer afraid." Upon returning home, she collected herself and in silence asked for forgiveness for having sinned so much. In her mind, she decided that no man other than Amir would ever touch her. She washed herself by rubbing her skin vigorously as if to empty her memories of the sexual acts she had had with other men. She rubbed herself until she felt pain. It was necessary to have a new skin, to become a lady worthy of being the wife of Amir, an excellent man, and a good and generous man. She spoke to her body as if it were another person: From now you will be wise, no acrobatics, no vice, you will certainly give pleasure, but without going crazy! Scarcely had her self-rebuke ended when she felt a desire even stronger than usual. She laughed and went to the doorstep.

Nabou felt a cool breeze in her hair. She turned and saw Amir, dressed all in white, stretching out his arms. No more fear, no more worries. She rushed toward him, put her head on his shoulder and rubbed against him. She felt his penis harden. She gently stopped Amir and told him to join her right after her bath. She wanted to give herself entirely to her husband without any reservation or restriction, as if it were her last night. Her skin shone under the moonlight. She had perfumed herself with the essence of a rare flower that she called "Desire." Naked under the cover, she waited for her master. No more storms, no more clouds on the horizon. She felt soothed and at the same time feverish. Her body was already trembling with the anticipation of the pleasure she was about to give and receive. It went up from her toes to the roots of her hair. She smelled good; she felt in harmony with her own self, reassured, ready to share everything. Amir, who had just turned fifty, was consumed by a desire of exceptional strength. He also had the impression that this night would not be like the others, that it would even be a fatal night, beautiful, enigmatic, sensual, crazy, perhaps a definitive night. He was frightened for a moment, then pushed off with his hands this fear and saw only the marvelous ass that was in front of him, clearly showing the red vulva with a few hairs around it as the guardians of an impossible beauty. His erection surprised him, for in all his life he had never felt a desire of such power as on that day, facing Nabou's body. She didn't speak, but her body moved to invite certain caresses that Amir was eager to give to satisfy her. No movement was inappropriate or disagreeable. Nabou led the dance with amazing ease, giving incredible pleasure and receiving as much, if not more. They then took their time to make love for a long time, holding back the moment of orgasm. Nabou reached orgasm several times, but she didn't let him know so that he could keep his erection as long as possible. To try to control himself, Amir thought of the white wife who gave him so little pleasure. Conjuring her image calmed him for a few seconds, and then he plunged more deeply into the ecstasy that this superb creature provoked in him. He took her into positions he came up with. Nabou's body, with its magnificent suppleness, gave itself with vitality and elegance to Amir's fantasies. It was as though an invisible being was guiding them and telling them that they were going through an experience they would never have again. The voice said: "This is your night, unique, irreversible. A night granted by death, which ensures that your pleasure multiplies to reach the peak of the highest mountain. There, where saints and fools unite to recite the purest, most precise, most powerful poetry—indescribable, impossible, as the beginning of the last journey, perhaps the most wonderful or the most terrible."

They fell asleep entwined in each other's arms like children. It was a nice fatigue, that of an unforgettable night. In the morning, Nabou went out to buy some fruit and flat cakes and prepared breakfast. She dipped a finger in the honey jar and put it in his mouth. She fed him with great attention, kissing his hand several times. She didn't eat, said she was waiting to feel hungry. Then, she walked out naked to the courtyard and washed herself using large buckets of water, which she let flow down her body while singing. The neighbor watched her without saying anything, but one could see in her eyes all the jealousy of the world. Nabou couldn't care less. She felt strong. Nothing could affect her anymore. She approached her man and confided to him in a strange and sweet way: "You know, I am not like most Senegalese women; I feel completely free in my thoughts and actions. My father was a Muslim, born in the Diola ethnic group in the town of Ziguinchor in Casamance. He served in the French army. At that time, recalled my old uncle, France had promised to grant independence to this country, but they did not. My father died for France. From my mother's side, I am a

Peul. My poor mother is worn out, affected by life's trials and her numerous pregnancies. As for me, I am here, in your arms, ready to follow you to the end of the world!"

She chose this moment, after her bath, to ask Amir to convert her to Islam. Astonished but happy, he took her hands, kissed them, and then began to recite the verses of Fatiha, the first sura of the Koran. Then, he listed the five pillars of Islam and explained what they stand for. He instructed her to repeat after him the words of the Shahada*: "There is no God but Allah, and Muhammad is the messenger of Allah."

Amir then explained to her what this religion's values consisted of:

"A Muslim must not believe that there are many gods; God is unique, powerful, and merciful. To be a good Muslim, it is enough to believe there is one God and Muhammad is his messenger; one must not kill, steal, lie, betray, cause harm, believe in Satan and in his henchmen; it is necessary to help the poor, to give alms, to pray, to go on the pilgrimage to Mecca when we have the material and spiritual means. In short, you have to be good and never cause others any harm. It is a constant battle against temptations."

She lowered her head and whispered:

"This Islam is not the one I know. I know that a woman is not the equal of a man, and that, for example, she inherits only half a share while the man has her double . . ."

"Listen, Nabou, we must not confuse Islam with the Muslims. The important thing is to behave correctly and humanely. He who mistreats a woman doesn't need the pretext of religion to do it. But I know that some justify their evil deeds by referring to Islam. They are wrong. All I can tell you is that I promise to love you and offer you the best I have. As for inheritance, the inequality is real, it dates from the time when women did not work."

Nabou retorted:

"And Khadija? Didn't Muhammad work for her before they got married?"

Amir smiled:

"You are well informed, it seems."

Moved, Nabou put her index finger on her man's lips and soon they let themselves indulge in romantic reveries.

Amir was happy, very satisfied by such a young, intelligent, and beautiful woman, and he started realizing that he had never felt this way about Lalla Fatma. Their marriage took place according to the rules of tradition. They had not chosen each other, and in spite of that, they had to love each other, that is to say, to do what the family expected of them: have children. Amir had not deviated from this rule; his wife had become pregnant within the first three months of their marriage. Did they love each other? One did not ask such a question. Morality was respected. Amir's business was going well, and Lalla Fatma reigned as undisputed mistress over the house and the children's education. No festivity, no family invitation was ever missed. The tradition was perfectly followed. Nothing should get in the way of this organization, established for centuries. In this city of Fez, closed within itself, the crucible of the Arab-Andalusian civilization, one did not joke with respectability. Amir was the husband of Lalla Fatma. Lalla Fatma was his wife. There was no doubt about this union. The proof, they had never argued. Was it love, for that matter, this quiet harmony, and this respect for each other until death? No one would be allowed to disturb this family order. As for love, one watched it in Egyptian films overflowing with clichés.

For the first time, Amir thought that there might be another way of living, and he realized that his feelings for Lalla Fatma were very different from those he felt in Nabou's arms. His life suddenly seemed to be turned upside down. He decided not to ignore his impulses and his passion. Amir in love! His friends in Diwane would have laughed at him if he had spoken to them about this sensation, which he experienced for the first time. He had never said "I love you" to any woman, nor offered flowers or expressed his feelings. That's how his strict education wanted him to be. His weaknesses were not to be shown in front of a woman. To be in love was considered a weakness, a sort of anomaly.

As time went by, Nabou continued to make Amir's heart feel very light. But he began to neglect his business. It was the local traders who reminded him that the goods were not on hand and that they had to be ordered from Cameroon, and sometimes from India. He thanked them and asked to be excused for being late and said: "Do as usual: cumin, coriander, ginger, turmeric, chili, *ras el hanout** with dead flies, pepper, cinnamon, clove, cardamom, and especially not curry; the Fassis detest this spice. And if you find saffron, put it aside; I'll take it with me in an airtight box . . . As for the quantity, you know it, I trust you!"

Nabou tenderly hinted that it would be more prudent for him to continue taking care of his orders himself. She didn't trust these people, said that too much goodness was interpreted as a sign of weakness and that he risked being ripped off by them. Then a discussion took place between them. She told him that he was wrong not to be careful of these traders and that it was naive to believe that all Africans were good and honest: "They are like everyone else: among them there are certainly honest people, but there are also a lot of dishonest people; you should check the merchandise when it is delivered to you."

Amir took her advice as proof of her love. He drew Nabou to him and kissed her, saying, "Thank you, thank you, Nabou, for caring!"

After several days spent in intimacy, Amir brought his son over and introduced him to Nabou. Both seemed intimidated. The house Amir had built was large enough for Karim to stay with them.

Karim had only one reaction. He opened his arms wide and said:

"Welcome . . . to . . . to the family!"

A few days later, when her temporary husband proposed to take her to Gorée Island where he was going to see a supplier and visit a great sage, she refused to go. This was the first time she dared to disobey her man. He looked at her tenderly and realized that something was bothering her. He placed his hand on her bare shoulder and asked her to confide in him. After a moment's silence, she burst into tears: "If I go there with you, I will die; I am so sure of it that I can't sleep. My ancestors keep repeating to me not to go to Gorée, because my great-grandfather's soul is imprisoned on this island in a well where slave traders had thrown him. I can free his soul only by staying close to my tree. I must speak to the tree, speak until I feel his soul, freed, flying to heaven. As long as I don't get this justice done, my great-grandfather will continue to suffer over and over again."

Amir didn't insist, and he asked her to wait for him. He told himself that she had not yet understood the meaning of the Muslim religion, but he respected her fears and her desire to liberate the soul of an ancestor. Karim was fascinated to witness the force of Nabou's conviction. At the same time, he discovered a universe of belief far removed from his own. With his son, Amir left for Gorée. Upon arriving on the island where his father was to introduce him to Hadj Mabrouk, a wise old healer, Karim was very impressed by the luxurious vegetation. He didn't know the names of most of the plants that surrounded him. Amir pointed out to him a whole range of bougainvilleas that were as beautiful as those seen at the outskirts of Fez. As for the palm trees, they were shorter than those in Marrakech, but much denser. The baobabs, which he had discovered in Dakar, had a special presence there. Their trunks, so broad and massive, their branches forming fine hair over an immense head, gave to some of these trees the appearance of statues sculpted by nature. Amir said to him: "These trees are many centuries old, considered magic trees by Africans, objects of holiness that preserve the memory of the ancients. For some, it's the tree of life, for others, it's the place of all origins where lies the key to all mysteries." Karim was amazed. He asked his father why Moroccans didn't see themselves as Africans and didn't believe in this magic.

Amir informed him that this island, which had passed from the hands of the Dutch to those of the French and also the English, was the place of the passage of slaves to America. Some were brought from Saint-Louis of Senegal, others from Ghana. Visitors could still see some traces of this tragedy. Karim didn't understand why they harmed innocent people. Amir tried to reassure him and told him that as a good Muslim he condemned slavery.

"You know, an old wise man once said that you have to give thanks to God for inventing the horse, otherwise the Whites would have used the Blacks to ride on. Men have always liked to humiliate others, especially poor people, people of color, and defenseless people. This is how it is. Slavery has been a horror and it continues to exist in some countries, not officially, but in a disguised way. Moroccans don't feel African because they have white skin."

"To be Afri . . . Africans, we must . . . we must have black skin?"

"No, we, you and I, all our family, are Africans."

"Li . . . like Na . . . Nabou?"

"Yes, just about, my son!"

Hadj Mabrouk received them by reciting prayers and burning incense of paradise in a small silver candlestick. Taking Karim in his arms, he pressed him against himself, and then, after a few silent prayers, he said:

"This child is a gift from God, a light. You are lucky to have him. He is the meaning of life and the grace of love, and I have rarely seen such purity in a soul and in a body. This child is not disabled. I know, it's difficult for him to express himself, and he will always find it difficult to make himself understood through words, but he possesses more than words; he has an immense, good heart, and he sees better than anyone else. Yes, Karim sees with his eyes but also with his heart. He will never hurt anyone. But you must take care of him, protect him, and do not allow bad people to approach him. In any case, he will recognize them before you. So, have confidence in him. He will not get higher studies, but, better than that, he will be a man of beautiful and supreme goodness. His knowledge, he received it at birth. God offered it to him because he is not capable of learning everything like other children. Here, such children are sought after, because we consider them to be messengers of God. It's the others who are put to the test: you, the parents, as well as all those who live with him. Leave Karim with me today. It will be easy for you during your meetings, and I would like to discuss a little about life with him and all the mysteries of the universe. Come back this evening. I'll wait for you."

In the evening Amir found his son dressed in a beautiful *gandoura*, which one of the sage's daughters, Shadé, had offered him. He was happy and seemed calm. He had eaten very well and couldn't hold back a burp, followed by "Hamdoullah" to excuse himself. During that day he learned a lot, but he also taught the old man a lot. His smile was beautiful. Amir once again thanked God for giving him this child, whom he sometimes called "my angel."

Before leaving, Karim embraced the sage and, with his hesitant words, declared his passion for Shadé. Intimidated, she lowered her eyes and laughed. Then she took him by the hand and, in a more private corner of the room, pressed him close to her very tenderly. Karim, excited by the feeling of the girl's firm breasts against his chest, lost control and ejaculated under his *gandoura*. Feeling ashamed, he didn't know where to go or how to hide the patch of sperm that was quite visible. His father pretended not to have seen anything, passed his arm over his shoulder, and they walked away quietly.

After spending two days in Gorée, they returned to Dakar. In the boat they took on the way back, an old toothless woman, seated opposite them, was chewing a stick of licorice. From time to time, she spat on the ground without worrying about what people might think. Karim, who had been staring at her for a while, approached her. She said to his father: "Hide this angel, his light is blinding me!"

Nabou was waiting for them. They found her looking very pale. She was suffering from pain in her back because she had spent a lot of time under her baobab tree. She had not left it until she was certain that her great-grandfather's soul had finally been freed. But in exchange she would have to leave her city, go far away, and perhaps follow her man. The ancestors had ordered her to disappear, because the slave traders' traces were still perceptible and quite harmful. Their souls, corrupted by evil, had not left Africa definitively. But Nabou was at last at peace with herself, persuaded that her ancestors had permitted her unfaithful wanderings to be forgiven. She confided to her tree how much she regretted the relations she had had with other men in Amir's absence. It was because she was then persuaded that he would not come back. She had heard of these men from Fez who took advantage of the black women during their business stay and then left them without ever returning or sending a penny to those who had given them so much pleasure. Some women had become racists against all Whites in general. They said: "White is the color of cowardice."

Nabou didn't want to impose herself on Amir, but she would have liked him to offer to take her to Fez. Her eyes were very expressive, and Amir had learned to read what she could not say. For the first time, Nabou realized how strong her feelings for him were. As soon as she saw him, her heart started beating faster. But neither of them needed words to express this love. He too, for the first time, felt overwhelmed by a feeling that went well beyond the marriage of pleasure. This time things had taken a turn that he had not seen coming. A man of his generation and his social class, from the Fassi bourgeoisie, had never been in love. He had read stories about love and thought that this could only happen in books, not in life—at least not in his own life. He felt like a hero in love with his beautiful woman, and he surprised himself by composing poems for Nabou. He trembled as he wrote, felt his body grow lighter, as though transported by music from afar, which enchanted him and made him fall even more madly in love with her.

Nabou had almost no connection with her family. Her father had died for France during the last war. Her mother, overwhelmed, had to raise alone her many children, born of different fathers. As she had a beautiful voice, she sang at weddings, but that was not enough to feed everyone. Only Abdou, a half brother on her father's side, still lived in Dakar. He had six children and couldn't afford to help his half-sister, whom he saw very rarely. He was a mechanic who repaired trucks and tractors.

Now Nabou's life depended on Amir. She had too much pride to ask her man for help. She knew that he was good and generous, and she relied on his intelligence and his intuition. She had heard what some women were saying in the hammam about what happened to those who left with traders from Fez. They talked about sexual slavery, about humiliation, about contempt. Nabou couldn't imagine Amir behaving this way with her. Amir was a pious man and obviously without prejudices. She had confidence in him, even if she never asked him about his life back in Fez. She knew he was married and had four children, Karim being his youngest. The ancestors had warned her against men in general, and the Whites in particular, against their extreme greed, their hypocrisy, their arrogance. Yet she never had the impression that they were talking to her about Amir. She didn't think there were such flaws in him. He was not perfect, but Nabou believed in her intuitions. She would follow him with her eyes closed to the end of the world. She loved him.

Sometimes she had moments of doubt. She couldn't imagine what her life would be like if Amir were to offer that she go to Fez and live with him. She was divided between what was said in the hammam and his impeccable behavior. She preferred not to imagine anything and to be carried away by the present moment.

On his side, Amir envisaged for a while the idea of living in Dakar. He would quickly find an occupation there because he had a sense of commerce.

But he thought right away that it would be impossible for him to abandon his family, his guilty conscience would prevent him from sleeping. He saw only one solution: take Nabou with him, even though it would cause many problems and disturbances in his life in Fez. The white wives knew very well that their husbands were contracting the pleasure marriages during their stay in Africa. They closed their eyes, did not ask any questions, preferred this to the men going to see prostitutes with the risk of catching a venereal disease, but this tolerance had its limits. Amir was going to disturb this order and go beyond these limits.

When night came, Amir asked Karim to make his ablutions and pray with him. After a moment of reflection, he informed his son:

"I intend to take Nabou with me. I cannot leave her here alone. She needs to get out of this neighborhood and live. It will be good for her to have a change of air, and then, to be honest with you, even if these are subjects that a father does not discuss with his son, I'm very attached to her."

Karim never once looked his father in the eyes. He listened to him and said nothing. But he was proud that his father confided in him. He murmured softly: "Yes, Father."

After a long silence, he dared to, stuttering, ask the question that tormented him:

"Are you going to ma . . . ma . . . marry her? Ma . . . ma . . . rri . . . rri . . . age?"

"Maybe, my son . . . She is already a little bit my wife. I am a Muslim, and I will never allow myself to harm someone and to oblige her to live outside the laws. Nabou has been generous with me and it's quite normal that I be the same with her. She needs to be protected, cared for, and well treated . . ."

"And Maman . . . ?"

"We are Muslims, and as a just and righteous man, I can marry up to four women. Your mother will understand it; her father had two wives. They quarreled all the time, but he kept them both until his death."

"Yes, but they were white . . ."

"That didn't stop them from being at each other's throats all the time. Your mother is a wise and good lady; she will understand. In any case, I am counting on you to have Nabou accepted by the family."

"Yes, Father! I'll try."

Karim spent an agitated night thinking of the task his father had just given to him. Would he succeed in avoiding disorder and disputes in the family, he who detests conflicts? Would he be able to convince his mother to accept the new situation? He had doubts and asked himself many questions. He would have liked to have the talent of a good speaker and prepare a speech to calm the predictable tensions. But he felt that his anxiety further brought out his disability. He liked Nabou, but he knew things were not going to go easily. He remembered his mother's uncle, who had brought two black slaves from Ghana, two "Dada." They had been very badly treated, and even animals didn't know the kind of ordeal they had endured in his big house, where they were not only subjected to humiliation by the white women, but had been starved, mistreated, insulted, and beaten. Being servants without wages, being good at everything, exploited at will, abandoned by the trader from Fez who didn't say a word, these women knew that one day they would revolt and take revenge for so much racism and exploitation. So they worked secretly against the white wife, toward whom they felt a ferocious hatred, and had cast a spell upon her, which had turned out to be ineffective. As a child, Karim had often heard of such things. He had witnessed many disputes. The uncle was weak and didn't defend the "Dada." One day, the white woman planted a kitchen knife in the shoulder of one of the black women. Without any treatment, she had suffered much and was left to die. Since this moment there was less tension in the house, but the uncle felt so embarrassed that he sold the other "Dada" on a Thursday at the slave market, a place near the Achabine neighborhood. With the money, he left with his white wife for a pilgrimage to Mecca, hoping thus to wash off his sins and be forgiven for the evil deed he had done or had allowed his Fassi wife to commit.

Despite their repentance at the Prophet's tomb in Medina, despite their prayers and the invocation of God's forgiveness, they had not found peace anywhere. The black woman's ghost hovered over their old house at night. Nothing was going right. Persuaded that she suffered due to a curse from distant Africa, the white wife lost sleep and then her mind. The husband had prayed in vain, had the readers of the Koran come for psalmody, but nothing could be done. All the harm done to the two unhappy women, as in a tale from *The Thousand and One Nights*, had turned against the family. The children left the house, the father went bankrupt, and the mother was taken in by her maternal uncle, who had made a fortune in a kind of clay from which *rassoul* is made. Thus, the family was destroyed, and everything was scattered. The sages used the expression "dispersion," and they said: "It is the worst thing when everything is broken and scattered everywhere; the family is sacred, everything must be done to protect it, nothing should break it, nothing should be done that would move family members away from each other. A family is a cell that gives and perpetuates life. If it's struck by the misfortune of dispersion, it is the end!"

Karim was afraid of such an outcome even though Nabou seemed to him as someone really kind. He had a hard time imagining his mother's reactions. Blessed by her, he never contradicted her, always obeyed her, and didn't ask too many questions. Tradition did not allow for open conflict or confrontation. Each one had his own place and no one tried to analyze another's mind. Karim, in his heart, swore to defend both Nabou and his mother, to do everything to keep the family united and strong. He knew that it was within his family that he would make the most progress and be able to fight most effectively against his handicap. He wanted this security.

Having finally decided, Amir proposed to Nabou one morning to go to Fez with him. She pretended to hesitate for a moment, then replied that she would like to follow him and rushed into his arms.

Before leaving, she wanted to visit her brother. As she didn't want to arrive empty-handed, Nabou asked Amir for some money, which was exceptional for her, and instead of buying food or toys for the children, she decided to put the banknotes in a handkerchief that she slipped into her brother's pocket. He expressed his gratitude and said:

"So you're going with the Fassi. Be careful. These people don't like us. It's better that you know about it and take precautions. When they are here, they show their good sides. Once back in their country, everything changes. So many testimonies have been reported by travelers . . . Once there, you will become a double slave: at night, he will make you his wife of pleasure, and in the daytime you'll be the slave, the servant, the one who will do the most painful work. Everybody knows about that. So be careful. I will always be here if you ever decide to come back home. Another piece of advice, my little sister. I know that you can take care of yourself, that you became independent early, but if you can take money from him and put it aside, do not hesitate. Because sooner or later the white woman will want to have her revenge and will take advantage of a weakness in her husband to throw you out. She'll not make things easy for you. It's normal, because for her, you are a danger, the main danger. You are young, beautiful, and intelligent. So watch out! I can never tell you enough how much you must be cautious of the Whites!"

Nabou defended Amir by talking about his qualities.

"He will marry me and give me beautiful children. I don't want to leave without having your blessing, since you are the eldest, and I consider you as our father."

He took her in his arms, kissed her on the head, and said:

"You know, I have not done any higher studies, but I know one thing: Life has taught me something simple; we complain about racism against us by the Whites . . . It's true, they are racists, colonialists, arrogant, and humiliating. But, know one thing, we don't like them, either. We, too, are racists; it's normal, and we're not going to kiss their feet . . . Except that we, we don't have the means to go colonize them. Go, don't forget us."

This was the only time when Nabou asked herself: Is Amir sincere, is he really in love? But she decided to trust her instinct, her inner strength, and also her man, whom she couldn't imagine as a supporter of slavery. She was in love, and for her this was the most important thing. But her brother was not ready to accept that kind of claim.

Nabou didn't have an identity card. So Amir had a document written by a scribe, for a good sum of money, which would serve as a passport: Presumably born in 1936, the year of the incessant rain . . .

As the date of departure approached, Amir began to sense Nabou getting a little anxious. He wanted to reassure her, but Karim went ahead before him. He spoke to her with words he could hardly pronounce, but she understood the message:

"Don't worry, nothing bad will happen to you. I will always be there to protect you. My father is a good man, and he has strong feelings for you. At the beginning it may be complicated, but be patient. I will be there."

As he spoke, he pointed at his muscles, which made her laugh. She felt that she could count on his protection, or at least on his affection.

She said nothing. A tear ran down her cheek. She hugged Karim, who was also crying with emotion. Often, his deep sensitivity made him cry and laugh at the same time. He flexed his biceps and said, "Get up and have some coffee!" Their burst of laughter filled Amir with joy.

In the evening, accompanied by Karim, Nabou went around the neighborhood. She stopped in front of certain doors or shops. With a wave of her hand, she seemed to say goodbye, and she continued walking while explaining to Karim what she would miss:

"You see, I like this little church. It's simple and modest, and I often go in and spend time there. I pray, even if I am not Christian. I love its silence and coolness. Here's the hair salon whose owner gave me a table and a chair when I was a public writer. Unfortunately, he's not here today. I was told he got sick. I pray for him. Here's a bench where I used to sit with my cousins."

Upon arriving at the main square outside the city center, she pointed to the baobab, saying:

"There reside the souls of the ancients, those who show us the way of truth, those who give us the light that guides our steps."

Karim, feeling moved, caressed the trunk and uttered a cry of joy. After a moment, when Nabou had spoken silently to the tree, they left without saying a word.

Chapter 3

The caravan left early in the morning. The merchandise would follow later in a much larger one. Amir had told the caravan man that he wanted the journey to be pleasant and amusing. The man therefore anticipated frequent stops, during which tents were erected and dinner was taken around the fire. Karim watched the stars and sang quite badly. Despite Nabou's expectations, Amir abstained and shared his son's tent.

The journey to Zagora lasted a whole week. On the way the caravan man invited them once to eat at his place. He had a small house made of packed earth at the foot of a mountain, a few hillocks away from the road. It was a great moment of joy. Karim took the man's children to the nearest hill, and, as they didn't speak the same language, he explained to them with sign language the marriage of the moon and the sun. With his fingers, he mimed the brightness of the light. The stars were the result of this union. The caravan man's wife was quite a strong woman, a métis who had a Mauritanian mother and a Tuareg* father. She was dressed in blue. She decided to share with Nabou, whom she found too thin, her secret to have hips that are more substantial, to hold on to her man. She advised her on a diet: Greek fennel every morning, pure honey, millet mixed with other substances that she suggested without naming them. Nabou replied that her man loved her just as she was, and she didn't need to gain extra pounds. Then the woman warned her, because, according to her, all men preferred fleshy women. Nabou didn't contradict her and moved on to asking the woman about her life and her children. The woman told her that the boys were going to school, which was half an hour's walk from the house; as for the girls, she was preparing them for marriage at their puberty, making sure to give them richer food. Nabou knew about these traditions but didn't allow herself to criticize them, just mentioning that her uncle had saved her by enrolling her in the French school. The woman offered Nabou a bag of Greek fennel when they left.

The next day, during the journey, the caravan man explained to Amir how much the Mauritanians detested the Senegalese: "You see, we are Whites, Arabs, like you. They are slaves. The moment they see a European, they bend over backward." Amir told him that it was racism and that God had created people of different colors so that they could meet and know each other. Then he quoted the Koranic verse in question, but he didn't succeed in convincing the caravan man.

Zagora, a funny name. Amir, Karim, and Nabou discovered a flat city, and the people, as they were told, ate a lot of dates; they were very kind, peaceful, and humane. There wasn't any hotel except a big house, where a nice man rented rooms and even provided the wood to heat the water at the city's only hammam. After a week's travel, Amir and Karim were dreaming of it, but they had to wait until the next morning because afternoons were reserved for women. Nabou was glad to be able to go, but the hammam woman, seated in an armchair that looked as tired as she herself, gave her such a look that at once Nabou felt very uncomfortable. Yet the woman had fairly brown skin, maybe even black. When Nabou undressed, all the women stared at her as if she were an animal that was being exhibited in a circus. Svelte, tall, delicate, breasts like hard fruits, with a princess's gait, her gracefulness and casualness provoked in women a mixed feeling of fascination and exasperation. They wondered where such a creature could have come from, who had brought her to this place, what she came to do here . . . Nabou washed herself, taking all her time, and didn't utter a word. A fat black woman approached her and offered her a massage. She accepted and allowed herself to be massaged for at least one hour. When she left the hammam, she was as black as she was when she came in, still beautiful and splendid.

Karim was waiting to take her back to the house. Amir waited for her, after having a light wash and his ablutions.

While Amir and Nabou spent some time together, Karim went out for a walk in the city. He liked to discover places during the night. He feared nothing and knew himself to be safe; perhaps, as his mother said, "protected by some saint." But Zagora at night was deserted. Not a cat. Not a café. Nothing. Just the moonlight, which gave things a strange aspect, that of images that are seen in dreams. The asphalt and the walls seemed silver. The moist and fresh air brought a little joy and happiness to this night visitor in his aimless, pointless wandering. He walked slowly, turning occasionally to see if anyone was following him. No one. No noise. Not a shadow. So much solitude and empty space put him in a daze. He rubbed his eyes. Then, there appeared a small man, who came to him and extended to him a hand full of dates:

"I'm the fastest and most efficient date picker. I climb date palm trees in seconds, and my small size helps me hang on to the strongest of branches."

Karim listened, nodding his head. He ate some dates that the small man offered him and asked him a question (he spoke without stuttering at all):

"Where are all the people?"

"They're sleeping peacefully. Me, I am the guardian of their sleep, purveyor of their dreams too. I go past the houses and as soon as I feel or I hear a certain noise, I step in. This is a city where nightmares are not welcome. My role is to chase them off; I send them to Ouarzazate, the city of merchants and bandits, a mecca of scam and hypocrisy."

Surprised, Karim asked him:

"Why this city?"

"Because people of Ouarzazate despise the people of Zagora. I know this because when I happen to go there, I have only trouble. Some bad French people and the natives who are under their thumb run the administration there. They ask for bribes all the time. Me, I refuse. I wouldn't mind giving them dates, but they don't like them, saying they're bitter. Such idiots!"

"But how do you manage to chase off nightmares?"

"I just wake up the sleeper. It's that simple. I have to leave you now; I sense a slight disturbance on the northeast side. Farewell."

The man disappeared. Karim was convinced that he had fallen asleep and had dreamed it all. But how to explain the dates that he was enjoying so much?

Karim continued his walk. He came face to face with a black cat that was staring at him. He tried to chase it away, but the cat meowed softly, rubbed against his legs, and began to talk. That frightened Karim. That a man who picks dates told him strange stories, he was ready to accept. But that a black cat could speak, it worried him seriously.

The cat said to him:

"I am not one of those jinns who come out at night to scare the children. I am a cat who was raised at the palace of Pasha Zaoui in Marrakech. One day, to punish me, the pasha exiled me to Zagora, and it was in this city that I discovered that I could speak like you humans."

Karim, curious, could not help asking:

"And what stories can you tell me?"

"Oh, if I were to tell you stories, the night would not be long enough. According to your human calculations, I am one hundred and five years old; I am indestructible. I must admit that I am tired of this life of wandering in an abandoned city, neglected, where nothing of interest ever happens. No party, no wedding. As soon as you and your father entered Zagora, the alarm went off. Nothing to worry about, but your arrival is an event. The desert has been advancing toward the city. The dunes are also moving closer to the houses. Someday the sand will bury us. Before leaving, ask your father to pray for us."

Karim asked him to explain the reason for his exile by Pasha Zaoui.

The cat gave out a long sigh and said:

"You wouldn't have a cigarette, a blonde preferably? That's what helps me tolerate my condition and forget my suffering."

Karim told him all he had were dates.

"I hate dates. Prefer savory food. Anyway, here's the story. It's a complicated situation: I witnessed an incident that I should not have seen. The pasha was very fond of young girls. The tradition was that on the day before every celebration, a girl would be presented to him from one of the tribes that were under his power—a virgin girl, of course. Just before the Mouloud*, he received a girl of ambiguous beauty. Tall, slender, svelte, and she had beautiful skin. Enveloped in a huge burnoose*, she arrived shortly before midnight. Now, it was the moment when everything changed about her."

"What do you mean by that?"

"This person had the appearance of a young woman, with long and thick black hair, but in reality he was a boy dressed as a girl. When the pasha undressed him, he gave out a little scream, and then he drew the person toward him. Me, I saw everything: the young man had a small sex. He lay on his belly and the pasha was getting ready to take him, but he noticed my presence. Not only did he beat me, but also he asked his henchmen to throw me into the snake pit. I escaped death. I ran, and I jumped without turning around. In short, after a few hours I found myself on a deserted road, and I continued until the day when an English tourist had pity on me and took me with him in his carriage. Obviously, I didn't know his language, but I could see that he liked me. I had lost a lot of weight. Once we arrived in Zagora, he fell ill and died slowly. I watched over him, sleeping on his belly, until the arrival of some important people. They kicked me out. I felt a lot of pain and started to meow, to cry, but words started coming out of my mouth. I myself was stupefied. Since then I speak, I have discussions, and death doesn't want me."

Karim reached out to take him in his arms, but the cat leaped with great force and disappeared into the night.

It was a full moon, and, in this light, the strangest things began to appear normal. Karim was happy with this meeting with the cat. He continued his walk, wondering what was going to show up next. Nobody came out from behind the walls. He stopped in front of a date palm tree and decided to sleep there. It was warm and pleasant, as in his childhood. A gazelle, probably lost, approached him. As he stroked its neck, the gazelle lowered its head and then lay down by his side. A few moments later, a shepherd arrived, his face contorted. He limped forward and threatened the gazelle and Karim with his stick. As soon as the gazelle saw him, it started running and he ran after it, furious. Karim said to himself: "What will happen next?"

And then, like a thunder, a voice answered him: "You will count the stars until morning, and if you make a mistake, you'll be swallowed by the sand!" Terrified, he got up and began to quicken his steps as if someone was following him. He dared not look at the sky anymore and began to count his steps. Exhausted, he stopped and fell asleep under a date palm tree that bore no more dates. In the morning, a strong sun and the sound made by some horses awakened him. Karim thought he recognized the angry shepherd, and he got up to leave. He came across a water carrier who handed him a bowl made of earth and filled with cool water. He then started searching for the house where he had left his father and Nabou.

"What house?" asked the people whom he met. "There is only one big house, which belonged to the pasha of Mhamid. He died and is buried there, and nobody dares to enter the place. It is haunted by evil and harmful jinns. Let's hope that your parents didn't try to spend the night there."

"Why not?"

"The jinns have the power to turn them into snakes or goats."

"That's impossible. My father is cou . . . cousin of the Pro . . . Prophet. He can't . . . snake . . ."

He insisted on being led to this cursed house.

"Walk for half an hour. You'll see the first hill. Go past it, then you'll see the second one. Go up that hill and from there you'll see a gray building in a rather dilapidated state: that's the one. The doors are double-locked. No one will open it if you knock. You'll have to wait for the dark night to fall before the occupants will answer you. Good luck. Be careful; don't believe everything you see."

He could not wait until night and went in search of the caravan that had brought them here. Someone had seen a gentleman and a black woman. But they had left the city. Karim started running toward the route to Ouarzazate. A peasant took him on his cart pulled by two lively horses. Thus he managed to catch up with the caravan and his father, who was extremely worried. Amir wanted to offer some silver coins to the peasant, who refused them:

"No money! Just your greetings and your blessing, Haj!"

The father looked pale and had not slept. As for Nabou, she had dozed a little. Amir told Karim about their night filled with nightmares and terrifying noises. Someone had ordered them to leave the house and join a child who was running on the route to Ouarzazate. At the moment when the sun reached its zenith, the caravan descended on the side of the mountain, going toward a small oasis where they ate bread dipped in olive oil. Nabou stayed a little apart because she thought the father and son needed to talk.

Karim, still in shock from the night he had just passed, talked about jinns, about a talking cat and some shadows. One word kept coming back: "violent." To calm him down, his father smiled at him, caressing his forehead:

"In the strange house where we were, a snake came to talk to us. It seems that a strange beast bit a servant, and, since then, he turned into a snake at night. He said to us: 'I look like a snake, but I'm Doukkali, the guardian of the house. Don't be afraid, I don't bite and I do no harm; I'm here just to scare and distress you. But at daybreak, I take back my human form, and then, I become wicked, very wicked. I advise you to leave before it's light, and be like me, be wicked, as only wickedness and deep evil win in this crazy life!'"

Karim then asked how Nabou had reacted.

"She is more used to this kind of thing than we are. Nothing surprises her. She has an impressive inner strength. I don't worry about her. I am sure that once we are home, she will adapt and even please your mother. She is very intelligent. She was lucky to go to school and to learn languages other than that of her country."

"And what about Mamouche?"

"Like most women of her generation, your mother didn't go to school."

"And you?"

"Me? Only boys were sent to school. I was lucky to go to 'the school of the sons of notables.' In the morning we studied French, and in the afternoon, Arabic."

Karim repeated the word "violent" again. He felt less confident than his father and dreaded the conflict that might occur between Nabou and his mother. He wondered why the snake had advocated wickedness. Why would evil be better than goodness? His father understood his astonishment and explained to him a theory he himself had experienced in life:

"Wicked people live longer than others simply because nothing affects them. Their selfishness and insensitivity preserve them. Their bodies are resistant, because they know neither disappointment nor vexations. They cause harm and don't fear retaliation. Their strength comes from their indifference, from their inhumanity. No goodness, no pity, no kindness. Being mistrustful, they anticipate and agitate before others even have time to get to them. Obviously, these are people who cultivate the appearance of civilized beings, but we must not trust them. Often they die in their sleep, very old. Their wickedness allows them to be in good health, as if the viruses, the diseases, avoid their inhospitable flesh. So that's why, in my opinion, the snake man advised us to be wicked. But neither you, no, especially not you, nor I, nor Nabou, are capable of meanness. Too bad, but it doesn't matter. Life is more beautiful with our flaws and our weaknesses."

The caravan took the road again when the sun's rays became more bearable.

At that time, Ouarzazate resembled a big village with a few houses and a small hotel for travelers. When they arrived, they saw bright lights in the distance, and they heard some music. The village was having a fair and a circus. It was a big attraction for the whole region. People were coming from neighboring villages to attend. All around, tents were set up. Amir rented one.

The show began. Piercing music cracked the air. Dwarves came on stage somersaulting. A ringmaster dressed as an American soldier announced the appearance of Lalla Khenata, "the most seductive, the most beautiful, the most wonderful of dancers from the South!" After a drum roll, a woman with long blonde hair appeared; when she turned around to face the audience, spectators saw the face of a man with a few days' beard and a big mustache. On top of his shirt he wore a kaftan full of sequins in bright colors. His husky voice and feminine allure gave a funny impression. Amir knew this fair that went around the country. He explained to his son and Nabou this disguise:

"A woman who respects herself does not perform on the stage, in public, so they hire men. They know how to dance and sing like a woman despite their deep and masculine voice. It's strange, but no one is fooled. There are even some who prefer them to real women."

Karim had trouble understanding this. From time to time he switched off and could no longer make sense of what was being said to him. The fatigue and inexplicable events of the night before had exhausted him. His speech became more hesitant; he needed rest and calm. But even so, he was curious to continue watching the show. When his father suggested that he return to the tent, he refused.

A hawker was selling lottery tickets by shouting: "Terrrrbahh; terrrrbahh!"* Several monkeys were fighting over some bananas on the stage, the spectators were applauding, all was well, it was fun, and the desert was far away. Karim found his childlike soul again. He was convulsed with laughter. He was happy. His father bought him a lottery ticket. It was the magical number 777. Karim was sure of winning. The wheel turned and then stopped at 555. He was fooled by superstition. He muttered: "No big eal," forgetting to pronounce the *d*.

With all that noise and excitement, it was hard to find sleep. Nabou, however, had no problem falling asleep. Amir asked his son, who wanted to spend the night under the beautiful stars, not to go too far away from their tent. Karim came across a dwarf who approached him jiggling her small breasts, and then she winked at him crudely. This made him laugh, and the dwarf squealed and ran off. The night was short. The caravan man woke them up early. It was necessary to take advantage of the cool air of the early morning to be on the road.

While leaving Ouarzazate, Amir met Ghazouani, an energetic trader from Fez whose shop was right across from Amir's in the Diwane district. He seemed worried. When Amir questioned him, he told him that troubles were brewing in the country, a kind of uprising against the French. Rumors spread everywhere about a group of nationalists who claimed Morocco's independence and the departure of the French. This wealthy trader was worried about the disturbances on the horizon. He said it straight out:

"The demonstrations will be the death of our business. Can you imagine, hordes of people shouting against the Christians? It'll force us to close our shops. I'm leaving for Guinea but don't know if, on my return, I will find my store as I left it. There are nationalists but there are also looters and thugs from the countryside . . ."

While speaking, he was looking at Nabou. He winked at Amir and said: "Be careful, they'll take her away from you!"

Amir didn't answer him, but anguish gripped him: And what if Nabou left me? She might follow a richer, more powerful man once I get her out of her precarious situation . . . He felt a pinch in his heart, and then an exchange of glances with Nabou was enough to immediately drive such a possibility out of his mind. Later, before falling asleep, he asked himself: Is she in love with me? He then pulled himself together and thought: I have never asked myself this kind of question about Lalla Fatma.

He thought of his cousin, Hafid, a rebel and anarchist who said that we must take advantage of the royal family's exile to end the era of monarchy that was ruining the country! He was the only one to speak this way. He knew this and repeated over and over again that the Moroccans had a golden opportunity to set up a democratic system like the one in Sweden, but that they were too cautious and lacked audacity and imagination.

Amir had tried to reason with him several times, but in vain. Hafid was, as he called him, "a hothead, a madman who was going to have problems and cause trouble for the whole family." As a cautious man, Amir controlled his nationalistic feelings. Already in 1930, when the French administration launched the Berber Decree (Berber Dahir), which planned a different legislation than the current one for the Arabs, Amir had followed his father at the head of a large demonstration where everybody shouted the same slogan: "We are all Muslims, we are all Moroccans." France wanted to protect the Berber tribes, the first inhabitants of the country, from Arab and therefore Muslim influence. France had planned Franco-Berber schools, a jurisdiction privileging the customs of these tribes, hoping thus to divide Morocco, which at the time had a majority of Berbers. Amir remembered this mobilization that had pushed back colonial France. It seemed quite natural to him to claim the independence of his country.

In 1947, he made the trip to Tangier to attend the speech of King Mohammed V, who officially demanded the independence of the country. Amir had joined the Istiqlal party and paid his membership dues regularly. His neighbor, Ghazouani, a selfish and greedy man, cared little about independence: what interested him mainly was to make money and go from time to time to M. Prosper's brothel, which was called "Bousbil."

The arrival in Marrakech was nerve-wracking. Gendarmes and soldiers were stopping carts and trucks to inspect them. Never had Amir experienced such humiliation. He understood then that Morocco was going to become a zone of political unrest.

The caravan man dropped them at the bus station on the Jemaa el-Fna Square. They had to wait several hours before getting on a bus that still had a French license plate. A Berber had bought it from a Lyonnais company that had used it for tourists. While waiting, Amir took Nabou and Karim to visit the beautiful Koutoubia Mosque, which, he told them, had a twin sister in Seville called the Giralda. To get to the mosque, they took a horse-drawn carriage. Karim sat next to the carriage man and told him about their trip. He easily confided in people, and he was never wrong about them: he knew whom to trust and whom to ignore. His father, meanwhile, explained to Nabou the city's structure and the importance of Pasha El Glaoui, who ruled as an absolute master of Marrakech and a large part of Haouz.

Having given a good tip, Amir and Nabou were able to get seats at the front of the bus. Karim chose to sit at the very back. From time to time he liked to retire into his bubble. He had a great ability to get away from the world and thus go into his secret daydreams. His father knew not to disturb him when he wanted to isolate himself.

The bus driver was loudly announcing to the passengers:

"Marrakech Casa, Marrakech Casa, departure in one hour, express bus, arrive in Casa in only one day, hurry, there are still some seats left . . ."

Through the window, Nabou watched the immense Jemaa el-Fna Square: musicians, dancers, acrobats, fortune-tellers, snake charmers, a tamer of a monkey that smoked cigarettes, a water salesman, women riding bicycles, beggars, kebab sellers, and even some black storytellers wearing traditional clothes.

Both the driver and the mechanic had their heads under the engine hood. A bad sign. Amir dreaded what often happened: a breakdown. After quite some time, the mechanic announced that the bus would not leave until the next morning because the repair required a missing part that only Hmida the One-Eyed, the famous blacksmith, a former butcher, was capable of making. A boy was sent to look for him at his place. He lived in the medina, and in the afternoon he liked to take a nap with his second wife. It was out of the question to disturb him. Hmida liked to be difficult and make his customers wait. He boasted that he used to be a mechanic in the French army, where he learned to completely take apart and reassemble a vehicle's engine. He lost an eye in the Atlas while doing this work. He divided his passion between women and his second job as a blacksmith. He worked little as a blacksmith, but as a mechanic, he often had his hands full. The boy begged him to hurry. In a bad mood, he followed the boy while insulting the manufacturer of this bus, which was constantly breaking down. On the way, he stopped in front of his son's shop that sold kebab meat. He reminded his son that they had an appointment with the village chief regarding an authorization to expand the shop. He said: "Don't forget to send him the sheep that I slaughtered yesterday. No gift, no authorization!"

Amir started looking for a hotel nearby. He didn't have to search long since there was only one, which was located near the square and had the fabulous name of Hôtel de la Jouissance. Another way to call it is *hôtel de passe**.

Karim had gone to the square and was probably going to spend the night in this mysterious and shady world.

The hotel manager was suspected of tampering with bus engines in order to display the "NO VACANCY" sign. Impressed by the appearance of Amir, who was accompanied by a young black woman, he decided to give him the best room, the one where there were fewer fleas due to Fly-Tox, the strong and unpleasant odor of which permeated the room. In spite of that, there were flies, and also, said the manager, nothing could be done, as they were smarter and more intelligent than the nasty fleas that fed on the customers' blood. It was clear the flies came from the countryside, as they were big, black, ugly, greedy, and particularly stubborn. They were a bad influence on the small, silent, city flies.

The bed looked like a hammock. It was sunken, as if there was a hole in the middle. Nabou decided to sleep on the floor, leaving the mattress to her man. In the adjoining room, a couple was making a lot of noise, and the woman was screaming. They were cries of pleasure. Nabou wasn't comfortable and tried to make Amir understand that she didn't want to make love in this room. She said:

"I'm used to sleeping on the floor; it's no big deal. It's you who brought comfort to my life, but at any time I can return to my former condition. This is the first lesson our ancestors teach us."

"Yes, I know, but it will also be necessary to prepare yourself to deal with Lalla Fatma, my first wife. She is someone who has a lot of class and qualities, but she is nonetheless a woman who will no doubt express her disagreement and jealousy."

"Of course, I would think so. But don't worry."

Though Nabou fell asleep right away, Amir fell victim to reflections that tormented him. It was in his nature to worry. He lived in anticipation of what might happen, and he suffered from it. He was weak, and he knew it. He wanted to foresee how things would go. So he imagined how things would be when they arrived home, imagined the reaction of the neighbors, the family, and finally Lalla Fatma's attitude. He put on one side those who would disavow him in all their hypocrisy, and on the other those who would say nothing. He could imagine how his uncle, the one who mistreated his two black women, would react. He didn't fear his judgment, but he had no desire to discuss with him his life choices. He could imagine the reaction of Saadia, Lalla Fatma's sister, a bitter and jealous old spinster who devoted herself to prayer and meditation. She said bad things about everyone, even people she didn't know. It was a great pleasure for her to discuss people's defects. She often pled with Allah and his Messenger to punish those whom she considered unworthy of the Muslim religion.

He was also afraid that one of his children, too attached to their mother, would be disrespectful toward him. But it was very unlikely. He imagined scenes where everyone would start shouting, or chasing Nabou away with sticks. He imagined himself, standing between his wife and Nabou, protecting her from hostility. When black women came to Morocco as slaves to labor away without protesting, white wives tolerated them—even if they knew that they also served to calm the sexual ardor of their husbands. But Nabou was not a slave. She was a woman with whom Amir had fallen in love, and he wanted her to be accepted by the family. She was neither a slave nor a servant, but a lady, beautiful and dignified, deserving respect and consideration. He told himself this and then sighed, knowing that the reality would be merciless for this woman and their love.

Amir decided to have Nabou stay in a kind of studio, a guesthouse called a *massrya**. It was where his father retired when he needed calm to read precious manuscripts. The *massrya* was ideal for that. There was a small desk, a bed, and some large cushions. This place would be perfect for Nabou while he prepared his wife for her arrival. He said to himself: She will not be jealous of her beauty since, for her, beauty can only be white. But she won't be able to bear seeing how much I am attracted by this young woman, that I will treat her with the same respect as I do her; that will be the heart of the problem.

He visualized these scenes one by one and was convinced that things would not go smoothly. He could not rely too much on Karim, who, despite his natural goodness, was incapable of upsetting his mother. He said to himself: First the gifts, then the rest, and after a few days, the presentation of Nabou, the beautiful, the sublime Nabou.

Early the next morning, the hotel manager knocked on their door. The bus had been repaired. Hmida the One-Eyed was having his breakfast on the square. He was eating a steamed sheep's head and sipping glasses of very sweet mint tea with it.

Karim was waiting for them at the hotel's entrance. He took Nabou's bag and started going toward the bus station.

The driver looked awful. The mechanic had spent the night alongside Hmida to assist him. The engine was making a sound like the cry of a camel or some injured animal. A passenger thought the engine was announcing to people the destination: MarrakkecheeCaza! The bus reversed. A chicken vendor was screaming. Two of his roosters had escaped. The passenger sitting next to Karim on the left row had bought three chickens, one of which was so thirsty that it would soon die. Just behind him, a somewhat tipsy soldier smoked "Troupe" cigarettes that smelled like burnt oil. Nabou put a scarf over her head and fell asleep. Amir took his rosary and started telling the beads automatically while thinking of something else. He felt a strong desire to make love with Nabou. It was obviously neither the place nor the moment, but he couldn't calm his urge, especially since she had placed her head on his shoulder and her breasts touched his arm. He drove out of his mind Satan who harassed him and began reciting in his mind a sura from the Koran. The recitation of some verses had a radical effect on him: no more irrepressible desire, no more excitement, and, above all, no more untimely erection on the bus, where he felt suffocated by the heat and cigarette smoke of the soldiers on leave.

The bus was going slowly and often stopped. The mechanic regularly opened the hood to cool the engine. Beggars took the opportunity to get on the bus and lament their fate. Amir always offered alms. It was the duty of every good Muslim. The soldier behind him wasn't the only one to smoke. With the heat, the air became unbreathable. The trip was a nightmare, especially for Amir and Karim, who were less used to high temperatures than Nabou. The townspeople couldn't tolerate the peasants' odor. They saw them as primitive people, dirty and rude. The people of Fez considered themselves the guardians of culture and civilization, and they felt that other Moroccans were not as refined as they were. It was a form of racism, a rejection of people from elsewhere; their ways were seen as coarse, and their clothes smelled of earth and cow dung. The experience of public transportation provoked in Amir and those like him a discomfort that he dared not express. In any case, he knew that it would be useless to protest because his neighbor had not washed himself or because someone was blowing smoke into his eyes. He always heard his father talk against Fez, which, for the rest of Morocco, was "the city of cities." Shutting themselves away, possessing a strong sense of their traditions, they left the old city only to go to Mecca or some of them to Senegal for trading. The rest of the time, they quietly worked on their small gardens, turning their backs on the rest of the country. The country people didn't like them, either. Often their wives or daughters worked as domestic servants in Fassi families. It seemed like slavery, but it didn't shock anyone. From time to time there was a tragic event, followed by a revolt against the mistreatment. The master of the house then intervened and everything returned to normal. But everyone remembered the tragic case of the Kohen family, the Andalusian Jews who converted to Islam during the time of the Inquisition. Mme Kohen's throat was slit during her sleep by one of her servants. Her husband was on a trading journey. The murderer turned herself in to the police, and she was quickly tried and sentenced to life imprisonment. Since then, the masters locked their bedrooms before going to sleep.

The bus stopped in front of a meat stand that was selling kebabs. With one hand a man shooed away flies, with the other he took care of the fire. A cloud of smoke covered his face but not his screaming voice: "Fresh camel meat! Delicious ground meat!" Karim was asked to bring Amir and Nabou bread stuffed with very spicy meat. They ate with gusto and drank big glasses of mint tea. It felt almost like a feast, but a few hours later, Amir's stomach being too delicate, he threw up everything he had eaten. The driver stopped the bus, made Amir get down, and let him vomit for as long as he needed. Nabou had no digestion problems and was discreetly amused. When the bus set off again, Amir was pale. He put his head on Nabou's shoulder and fell asleep like a tired child.

Nabou was looking at the landscape through the bus window. She drifted off to her adolescent memories. At that time, her father, a native of Casamance, pampered her with each of her wishes. He told her not to pay attention to the mockery that people in this part of Senegal were victims of. He loved her very much and advised her to beware of men's greed. It was he who initiated her confession under the baobab tree and spoke to her a little about Islam, while warning her against Arab Muslims who, he said, "had no respect for women." Nabou had her own conception about spirituality, and, above all, she wasn't afraid of death. Her father knew he was going to die soon. He once said to her: "The captain always sends the Blacks to the front. We are fodder for cannons. But if I were to die, it would be the will of God and my ancestors." As for Nabou's mother, left behind by her husband who spent more time in the army than at home, she said to her: "I don't worry about you. With your body so well carved, with your almond-shaped eyes and your intelligence, you will have any man you want; all you need is to give him a look, a wink, and he will come as a lamb and put himself under your thumb. But be careful. Men are cowardly and rapacious. Don't give them everything right away; learn to keep them waiting. Be smart and never come home to me crying." She made things clear.

Nabou lived most of the time with her maternal aunt who had no children. Her husband was the village teacher. Nabou was at school all the time: she liked to draw, write stories, and read everything her uncle advised her to.

She was barely sixteen when she fell in love with this kind and attentive man. She was fascinated by his generosity and by his large, very fine hands. One day, she accidently saw him bathing. He was naked, thinking he was alone. His wife, a seamstress, had gone out. Nabou couldn't help watching this elegant, tall, and slender body. Her eyes stared at his penis and she found herself drooling. She experienced a strange desire accompanied by a hot liquid that ran down her legs. She put her hands on her pubis and began caressing. She had no idea what was happening to her. Then it became a habit for her, and every night before falling asleep, to calm her desire, she stroked herself slowly and methodically, remembering the images of this naked man who had so excited her.

The seamstress realized that the girl was not innocent. She made her talk and discovered that she desired her uncle. Her aunt explained that such an attraction for a man who was so close was not allowed, that her uncle was like her father, even if he was not from the same family. Nabou lowered her eyes and listened while crying. She decided to go back to live with her mother, but things went very badly there. One of her mother's temporary husbands wanted to sleep with her the moment he saw her. She fled from home, and, in the street near the school, she fell into the arms of the forbidden uncle. He was not a fool and asked her to follow him. He opened the school door, and it was in his office that he took her virginity. She was frightened by the blood and started to cry. The uncle reassured her while wiping her thighs and kissing her gently. When she got up, she had some trouble walking. He told her to stay there and rest, brought her lemonade, and left her alone. What happened had to be their secret.

For more than a year, they met in this room and made love on uncomfortable mats. Nabou's allure and attitude changed, which didn't go unnoticed by her aunt. One day, she woke up with an alarming thought: "If Nabou gives him a child, I'll be damned! This relationship must be destroyed."

She had no way of putting pressure on her husband. At the slightest argument, he would leave her. There were many more women than men. She sought help from the blind wizard, who told her that he could do nothing for her. Miraculously, Nabou didn't become pregnant.

One day, while she accompanied her aunt to the fabric market, Nabou bumped into a stranger, a Muslim man dressed all in white. He spoke to her as if she were a child who was lost in a labyrinth:

"Hey, where do you come from? You seem to be lost. You need a master to take care of you; so much beauty should not remain without a protector."

The aunt, who was listening to Amir, was happy to encourage her to follow this man. It was an opportunity to keep Nabou away from her husband:

"I'm not her mother. I'm her aunt, but she's like my daughter. She needs to become independent. Her father isn't alive and her mother, who sings at weddings, can't make ends meet."

Nabou didn't say a word, but deep down she considered the possibility with interest. She was less and less in love with the uncle, and it was time for her to try a new adventure.

The stranger said to her:

"I would love to hear the sound of your voice."

"Yes, my lord!"

"Where did you learn to speak like this? With Molière?"

"Yes, my uncle is the director at the school. He's the one who has taught me a lot."

"I wouldn't like to distract you from your studies. They must be continued, but that would not bother me."

The aunt stepped in as though she were Nabou's own mother:

"What are your intentions, sir?"

"Good! Very honest!"

So it was that a few days later, Amir married Nabou, who was approaching eighteen, for a period of fifty-eight days. Clergymen had their offices at the entrance to the only mosque in the neighborhood. They drew up a contract mentioning the amount of the dowry, the kind of gifts to be given, and the duration of the marriage. They checked to see if the young woman was consenting and had Nabou sign her name at the bottom of the document next to Amir's signature. The two clergymen congratulated him on his first "pleasure marriage." Nabou and her "husband" went away holding hands, as though they had known each other for a while.

Amir first took her to a small, furnished house, and they lived there as man and wife until they would have their own home. During the first days, they struggled to find a balance. She didn't give herself completely to him; she let him caress her but didn't get into lovemaking. He was gentle and patient with her, but a little clumsy. Then one evening, the way she took things in hand produced a burst of joy and light that made Amir go crazy. He never thought a woman could give him so much pleasure. He discovered the beauty of her body that wrapped around him with suppleness and grace.

He began to recite verses of unknown poets, or perhaps they were his own. He was delirious, drooling, kissing her feet, licking her toes one by one, then putting his face between her thighs and trying to reach with his tongue the labia, the clitoris, the pubis, everything. He went crazy, screamed with pleasure, and then fell down with all his weight on this frail body gifted with infinite eroticism.

Nabou didn't speak and let him say whatever was going through his head. She was very happy to give herself to him and to hear him being delirious with pleasure. Her uncle had trained her perfectly. She had learned how to satisfy a man and how to succeed in keeping his erection inside her. She knew the art of barely noticeable techniques that had spectacular effects on him.

Amir asked himself if he would want to go back to Fez one day. When he remembered the intimate moments with the white wife, he wanted to laugh and cry at the same time. Why, he wondered, are our white women so fearful, so inhibited, so awkward, so timid? Oh, I know, we make love to procreate and not to enjoy our bodies to the point of madness. Until today, he had thought that sexuality was a cold and passive activity: his wife put herself on her back and spread her thighs, and it was for him to do the rest. Once he ejaculated, he withdrew, wiped himself with a small towel that his wife handed him, and fell asleep satisfied. Since he discovered this volcano, it seemed to him very difficult to return to the bed of his legitimate wife, the mother of his children.

Settat was a small town without much interest. The bus had to make a long stop to cool down the engine and allow the driver to sleep a little. There was no one out except a few beggars, who, alerted by the travelers' arrival, held out their hands to beg even though it was night. Everyone was fast asleep. Some snored or talked in their sleep. Dreams swirled around their heads. There was a strange atmosphere on the bus, as though the travelers had all been anesthetized. Karim once again found the ghosts of Zagora wrapped in huge, brightly colored fabrics. They danced like whirling dervishes, asking him to join them. As he got up, his feet got caught in a fisherman's net, and he found himself at the bottom of the sea struggling not to drown and die. He screamed and woke up. He didn't want to go back to sleep for fear of going back into this terrifying nightmare.

Karim was having a lot of nightmares. Nobody knew whether it was related to his disability or to his imagination that had no limits. His view of the outside world was clear without the least cloud. He saw what others did not even notice. On the day of his circumcision, women came to give him kisses and presents. He was very happy in spite of the pain. When Houda approached him, he pretended to be asleep so as not to be kissed by her or for him to smile at her. His mother, worried, asked him for explanations. He responded with a gesture with his hand that meant "not nice," along with a grimace that left no doubt about the meanness of this woman. His mother was very impressed: Houda was in fact a pest, a malicious gossiper, envious, a spell caster, and the devil's ally. Karim understood all this without ever having seen her before. Another time, a gypsy street vendor knocked on the door. He was selling fabrics that he claimed were imported from France. Lalla Fatma was about to be tricked but Karim walked up, felt the fabric, and then shook his head, adding, "Junk from Japan." There had been a large influx of poor-quality Japanese goods, so now everything that was ugly was labeled Japanese. Karim thus condemned the cheat's fabrics.

In the family he was considered "the sweet bread," "the pure heart," "the altar of goodness," "the innocent." Some loved him sincerely, others put him at a distance—the handicap, said his father one day, is not contagious, after all. It doesn't justify mistrust. Karim was above all that, and he was doing well. He had a heart murmur, so once a year he saw Doctor Adrien, who worked in the French army barracks outside the old city. Karim was still young when, one day, he accompanied his mother to the hammam; an old woman asked him to show her the palm of his right hand. She scrutinized it like a fortune-teller, and then released it, saying, "Never mind." Lalla Fatma didn't understand her reaction. The hammam attendant, sitting at the entrance, explained that this woman was looking for a child who had a straight line in the middle of the palm because she believed that children with such a line could find a hidden treasure. A band of thugs had recently tried to kidnap a little boy who was born with this line and wanted to sell him to a tribe in the High Atlas where they said there was treasure of all kinds. Lalla Fatma had cold sweats and took Karim by the hand and told him never to show his palm to anyone.

The air in Settat was hazy and heavy. The sky didn't have a natural color. It was sometimes white, sometimes gray. Karim sensed before everyone else that they should leave. The driver, whom he tried to warn, didn't understand what he was saying and made a gesture as if to say "later." But Karim was convinced that this place was going to experience something bad.

Indeed, a dust storm suddenly rose, accompanied by a very violent wind that nearly carried away everyone in its path. Karim, terrified, found refuge in his father's arms and began to cry like a child awakened in the middle of a nightmare. It was impossible to go elsewhere, so both the mechanic and the driver, who came from this region, went to have dinner with their families. All the passengers waited, hoping to see the two who were going to drive them to Casa despite these gray blasts. One of the passengers said: "It's no longer the Mahdi* who is awaited, but the driver!" Finally, they all slept in the bus, and early in the morning the two crazy men appeared looking tired and stinking of beer. When the bus started moving, people began to clap as if they had escaped a real disaster.

On the road, some police inspectors stopped the bus to check the passengers. They told the driver that they were looking for two thugs who allegedly murdered some Frenchmen in Meknes. Amir realized that these were nationalist militants fighting for Morocco's independence. Without reacting, he showed his papers as well as those of Karim and Nabou. The police made her get out and searched her. She let herself be searched without saying a word. She was the only suspect. This made her angry, but she managed to control herself. There would be no point in protesting, especially since she was no longer in her own country, and her ID papers were not totally legal. Amir gave a banknote to the mechanic, who put it in one of the inspector's pockets. Nabou was allowed to return to her seat. After talking with the driver some more, the inspectors allowed the bus to leave. The passengers made a few comments aloud and some began to sing the hymn of independence. The driver accompanied the song with a few blows of the horn to show his support. There was at last a nice atmosphere in this bus that had left Marrakech a long time ago and which finally made its triumphal entry into Casablanca, where other travelers were waiting to leave for Fez, Taza, and Oujda. The train station was filthy and cluttered with all kinds of things. There wasn't a single bench to sit on. A café offered a few dishes smelling of oil that might have been used several times. The buses left their parking lot in a cloud of black smoke that immediately filled the entire space. There were skinny and dirty cats, and a dog that was getting kicked from time to time. Beggars were roaming around. It would be necessary to wait for several hours before the Laghzaoui bus departed for Fez.

Amir couldn't think of going through Casa without visiting Hadj Habib, his maternal uncle, who had left Fez before the war and made a fortune in the wholesale trade. Amir liked him because he was a bon vivant*, a generous man and without prejudices. He was the only one in the family who had defended the two black women abused by his brother and by his white wife.

Amir had Nabou and Karim wait in a café and went to the big *kissaria** where his uncle's shops and warehouses were.

The moment Hadj Habib saw Amir, he exclaimed:

"You must have come back from Africa! It shows. You look as happy as a child on the day of the Ashura* festival. How's my little Karim? I love and adore him."

When he heard that Amir was indeed returning from his trip, he insisted that everyone in Amir's family come to his house and ordered his helpers to pick them up and take them home.

Hadj Habib was one of the first Moroccans to buy a Cadillac. He had ordered it from America and had to wait six months for it. It was his toy, his pride. From time to time, he let people he loved use it.

He lived in a beautiful villa in the residential neighborhood called Anfa. Everything was impeccable. Amir was happy to finally have a large bathroom. Nabou, too. They needed to wash and forget all the unpleasantness of the long bus ride.

Desiring to pray, Amir asked for the direction of Mecca, which Hadj Habib showed him. After dinner, they discussed the country's political situation. Hadj Habib helped the nationalists. Amir had doubts because frequent demonstrations and strikes were jeopardizing his business. His uncle advised him to help the nationalists and not show too much sympathy for the French.

The following morning, Hadj Habib woke up Karim, put him in his convertible Cadillac, and drove him to the coast for breakfast. Mad with joy, the child stood up in the car, his hair in the wind, and greeted the passersby as if he were the king. This made Hadj Habib laugh, and he promised him a gift.

Karim loved to eat. He didn't know how to deny or stop himself, but as he did a lot of sports, he didn't get fat. On their way back, Hadj Habib stopped in front of a stationery shop that was also a bookstore and asked to see some typewriters. They had only one model, the Italian Olivetti. He bought it and also got some reams of paper. Knowing that Karim had difficulties writing by hand, he said to him: "Now, you'll write to me one letter every week. But before you do that, I'll send you someone to teach you how to use the typewriter."

Karim was so happy that he gave Hadj Habib a tight hug and said: "You, I love!"

After two days of merrymaking, Amir decided to leave for Fez. There was no question of again taking the bus, known for breaking down and falling into ravines, or taking the train that never left or arrived on time. They would leave in Hadj Habib's truck that was going to make deliveries in Meknes and in Fez.

Amir and Nabou sat in the front with the driver. Karim and the driver's assistant made a comfortable place in the back among the bales of fabric.

The boy took out his typewriter and typed anything that went through his head. Overjoyed with this gift, Karim waited impatiently for an instructor to learn how to use it efficiently.

The trip was a bit long because of the many deliveries of Hadj Habib's merchandise. They had lunch in Meknes. There were many soldiers because the village of El Hajeb, a few kilometers from where they were, had a huge military barrack and a brothel that the driver and his assistant knew well.

The closer they got to Fez, the more Amir felt a tightness in his chest.

Chapter 4

The air was soft this morning. A little smoke left traces in the whiteness of the horizon. It was the moment when potters and bakers lit the ovens.

From a distance, Fez looked like a big white bowl covering other bowls. Fez captivated all those who went there for the first time. The roofs and the terraces were connected and drew an entangled arabesque that evoked daydreams among visitors from the farthest of lands. Fez had its smell, its own fragrance, an indefinable scent carrying the memory of all the perfumes spilled on its soil since the year 789, the date of its foundation by Moulay Idriss I, a direct descendant of the Prophet Mohammad.

The spirit of the city stretched beyond its borders. Fez glowed and spread its music throughout the country. This came close to disturbing people in neighboring cities. Time was entombed in Fez, the enchanted source of the Spirit, the refuge for the converted, and the divan for poets weaving their verses through the dark, narrow streets. It was also the center for trade, exchange, arbitration, and all the auctions for gold and silk. Everything was in its right place. That was the secret of this city. For the Jews, it was gold, gold threads, mattresses filled with raw wool. They had their own neighborhood, the Mellah*, just outside the medina. There was a little condescension by the Muslim Fassis, but no rejection and never any violence. No mixed marriage, either. The whole city remembered the incident that had nearly ruined the coexistence of the two communities, when Mourad, son of the theology professor Laraki, wanted to marry Sarah, the rabbi's daughter. The scandal made a lot of noise. The two lovers had to go into exile abroad, in France or Belgium. Both families were advised to forget the two children whose madness made them lose their way. It was as if they had never existed. Curiously, this incident created a relationship between the two families. The mothers saw each other secretly in the hope of getting some information about their children. Time passed, and then one day, without warning, Mourad and Sarah returned with a baby in their arms. It was this birth that reconciled the children with their families. But deep down there remained a feeling of regret expressed through sighs and disapproving looks.

Each trade had its own neighborhood. The city was organized rationally and practically. So, Amir had his shop in the Diwane, which was reserved for spice dealers. Fabric merchants were on the opposite side of the street. Further, the dried-fruit vendors were gathered in a courtyard that was also filled with many different kinds of birds.

Despite his worries, Amir looked forward to arriving home, to handing out the gifts to Lalla Fatma and the three children. The gift for his wife had to be in proportion to the shock she was likely to suffer. He bought her, at the *kissaria* of Casablanca jewelers, very fine gold bracelets. He knew she dreamed of them because hers were old-fashioned. He was nevertheless aware that the gift would not change how she would react to Nabou. There would be conflict, crisis and clash, cries and tears, moments of tension, and then everything would return to normal.

Upon arrival he realized that he didn't have the keys of the *massrya* where he wanted Nabou to stay for the next few days. He turned to look at her without her being aware. Her face didn't show any emotion. He noticed during his first trip to Senegal that Africans' faces were not easy to read, no doubt a question of culture or appearance that he couldn't grasp. Karim was clutching the typewriter against his chest. Amir decided to ask the driver to break the lock on the *massrya* door.

They arrived in Fez in the middle of the afternoon. The truck dropped them off at Batha Square, not far from a second entrance to the house that led directly to the *massrya*. They had to go through narrow, unpaved streets like in Ziate and Arssa Andalusia. The driver gave the door a shove with his shoulder, and it opened. It was a nice day; the trees had flowered. In the *massrya*, everything was in order, as though someone had prepared it. Nabou was made comfortable; Amir handed her a basket of food and asked her not to go out or open the door to anyone. There was no electricity; it needed to be switched back on. Exhausted by the journey, Nabou had nodded off on her feet. She lay down on the bed and immediately fell asleep. Amir was fascinated by her capacity to fall asleep so easily. She slept, a light smile on her lips, her large eyes slightly open. The truck driver's assistant carried Karim's and Amir's suitcases up to the main entrance of the house. Lalla Fatma had sent a maid to the rooftop to let her know as soon as she saw the master approaching. The day before, a messenger had come to inform her that he was about to return to the city. Amir and his son heard the welcome ululations, smelled the scent of paradise. Karim made a face; he didn't like this smell of incense, which was used both on festive days and for funerals. But today it was to celebrate. Lalla Fatma looked beautiful and was wearing her caftan embroidered with gold threads. With hardly any makeup on, she waited with calm and grace for her husband, who had left more than two months ago. Karim kissed her hands and snuggled in her arms. He showed her his typewriter. She approached her husband, took his right hand and kissed it. It was the custom. He placed his hand on her head, as though giving her his blessings. She leaned over him and made a gesture of kissing his shoulder. Then the children welcomed him. At a distance, Batoule and the servants bowed to wish them happiness. Dinner was ready. Lalla Fatma had invited some members of the family to celebrate the return of the master. This called for a party. There was the sister-in-law, Saadia, always mean and quick to badmouth others. She couldn't restrain her spitefulness:

"So are the Negresses, the Kahlouchates, still as black and dirty, with their smell of perspiration and bad breath?"

Amir didn't answer. She continued about another subject:

"And Karim, does he still stutter as much?"

At this point, Amir turned toward her and bluntly demanded that she shut up or else he would throw her out. He had already chased her out of his house once because of her indecent behavior. She realized that she had to stop and keep quiet. Also, Lalla Fatma waved at her to calm down. When in an evil mood, her eyes turned yellow and a little saliva ran down her lower lip, accompanied by a scowl. She was unpleasant to look at. In fact, she was pathetic, dry, and had no qualities.

Karim couldn't help mentioning Nabou. He used the words:

"Beautiful, Naaa . . . bou!"

Everyone wanted to know who this Nabou was. Amir replied that she was a person they had met and was careful not to reveal any more.

The incident was not over. Late in the evening, when he was in bed with his wife, she asked him calmly:

"Have you brought back a slave from Senegal? We already have two servants, three with the cook. She would be too many."

"No, not a slave. I have brought back a free woman. Following the precepts of our Prophet Mohammad, may the salvation of Allah be upon him, I contracted a marriage of *mut'ah**, a marriage of pleasure, with a young woman named Nabou. It's a pretty name, don't you think?"

"What can I say, my husband, my dear husband? God has given you men the permission to marry up to four women. I will not go against God's will. I could get angry, break vases, cause a scandal, cry, and even leave and go to my parents' house, but I am yours, very attached to you, and I don't want to lose you. I will do like all women who are forced to live with other wives. Provided that she never disrespects me. I am your legitimate wife, and I have the right to full respect. I don't want anyone to make comparisons between her and me. I have my pride. But I am a good Muslim. I obey God, and I belong to you. All those who have protested have lost everything, lost their homes, their children, their honor. I didn't go to school, but I know some verses of the Koran by heart, and I follow God's precepts and his laws. I will pray to God to preserve us from this foreign woman and protect our family. I hope she will remain an outsider, will she not?"

Amir was stunned by what she said. It seemed like she had been preparing these words for a long time. There is no doubt she had an intuition. It only remained for Amir to bring Nabou to the house.

Before making love, Lalla Fatma asked:

"I suppose you put her up in the *massrya*?"

"Yes, you have guessed right and understood everything. I am infinitely grateful to you. May God keep you well and give us both good health to accompany us as we get old."

This was a prayer that was recited when there were health worries. "May God give us health at our age," his wife repeated.

Faced with her calm and intelligent attitude, Amir lost his desire. It was impossible to have an erection. For the first time since their marriage, Lalla Fatma took her husband's penis in her mouth. He, too, had never kissed her vulva. Women said among themselves in the hammam that only sluts and whores did such things. Despite Lalla Fatma's efforts, his sex remained limp, felt no desire or pleasure. She held it for a moment in her right hand, tried to wake it up, then gave up. He gave her a kiss and said goodnight. The following day, he could not believe her daring of the night before. She was going to give him a blow job! What a good initiative! What had happened during those months of his absence for Lalla Fatma to dare to do what no Fassi bourgeois woman would, in principle, tolerate? Ah, it must be the hammam! A place where tongues loosen, where the stifling heat often helps women tell their stories freely without holding back. There was Samra, a divorced woman turned into a matchmaker. She gave advice to young women who were still unmarried:

"If you want to keep and hold on to your man, two things are essential: sex and food. You have to make him dependent on you for both. You must not give everything right away, but make him drool, languish, wait. Keep the mystery and don't say everything. Another thing, stop believing that black women's sexuality is stronger than ours. They are like us, except that they have understood that you have to be totally liberated, have no taboos, and no restrictions. This is what I advise: you must free yourself! Use your body to drive your man crazy. Remember, men are weak and not very courageous. Caress them everywhere, kiss them everywhere, and be open; like that your desire and theirs will only be stronger. As for food, you have to prepare some small dishes yourself that the cook doesn't usually make. Feed him, kiss him, lick him everywhere. That's the secret, my sisters!"

Then followed a discussion about men's genitals, their size, their thickness, their strength. Here, Samra was blunt:

"It's never the biggest that gives the most pleasure. It's a myth, and stop believing that black men are more virile than white. It's all in the head, not in the underpants. And I know what I'm talking about." A young wife said: "Negresses have no taboos, and men like that. That's why some have their clitoris cut." Samra corrected her: "No, they are freer, and their religion doesn't block them. And also, their traditions are different from ours." Another asked: "So why do our men go to Africa? They say they go to trade, but I suspect they go there to plunge themselves between the thighs of these Negresses, these thieves of husbands, thieves of their health!" She was angry because her husband had not only abandoned her, but also went to live in Guinea.

Lalla Fatma felt intimidated, yet very interested in what Samra was saying. After her last visit to the hammam, she went back home thinking: Now, I'll have to learn to free myself! It'll be hard!

Amir took his time before bringing Nabou to the house. No blunders, no mistakes, because any wife would be offended by much less than this. Lalla Fatma's words remained ambiguous for him. But tradition, certain privileges given to men by Islam, made the task easier for Amir, who sought to solve a very problematic situation: to live with two women under the same roof without any complication or annoyance arising from either woman. He knew he was hoping for the impossible. His wish was simple: he wanted to please everyone and not offend Lalla Fatma, while at the same time making Nabou believe that she was welcome in this house, even though everything could change from one day to the next and make everyday life hell. Impossible to believe that he would be able to avoid conflict. He hated conflicts, and all his life he tried to flee from them, losing on both counts. This was his temperament. One day, his elder brother said to him, "You are naive, that's why you will never make a fortune. You think that goodness will solve problems, but not at all: goodness is an illusion that makes you stupid and causes you to allow others to steal everything from you. So, please, enough of being naive; life is a struggle, not a nice picnic in spring, where everything is nice and everyone loves each other. Wake up. Look at how I work. If I'm not careful, my employees will ruin me . . . It's not a matter of becoming a bad person—that, that is not possible, but at least be realistic: if you hesitate, if you show a little understanding, you're screwed because you will be considered weak, and women don't like that at all."

Amir was a pleasure-loving man. He gave priority to pleasure and good food. In the morning he dawdled in bed while his wife massaged his legs. He neglected his trade and relied on others to take care of it. He was happy as he was and knew he could not change his character and his old habits. He also knew that his brother would never let him go down. Maybe, he said to himself, I should take evening classes to learn how to be mean, hard-nosed, strong, and finally I will be very unhappy.

Hell took a while arriving in the big house. At the beginning, especially on the first day, Lalla Fatma treated Nabou as a guest who would be leaving soon. She greeted her with kind words, but regularly hinted that she should leave soon:

"How long are you going to be here? A few days, a week or two?"

Nabou didn't answer, smiled, and then said something like: "Inshallah!" that did not make much sense in this situation. She remained dignified and proud. She controlled herself well and never got irritated.

Amir had her put in the guestroom, which was comfortable and had an attached bathroom. When he went away for a few days, Lalla Fatma took advantage of his absence and moved Nabou and her belongings to a corner in the kitchen. Using a calm but authoritative voice, Lalla Fatma made it clear that she had to sleep there. Right away Nabou sensed this woman's strength and understood that she wouldn't be able to resist her, and she felt weak and hurt, sensing that she controlled nothing.

"So, your place is with the servants. You're here to work, clean the house, wash clothes, iron, and follow my orders. You'll eat with the two village women who work in the house. As for the cook, Batoule, you won't go near her. In any case, you'll never touch the food. I know the Blacks have a strange odor. I know this smell. You, you'll go to the hammam every Thursday. That will be your only day off. Forget about going to the town and talking to people. Here, I'm the one who commands. I give orders to all, including my husband. So, everybody must stay in his or her place. Don't try to get too close to us, don't try to mix, and, especially, understand one thing clearly: you are not family; you are just a slave my naive husband brought back in his baggage. Another thing: when you speak to me, keep a distance from me and don't raise your eyes at me."

After a moment, while Nabou had her eyes lowered, the white wife asked:

"Have I made myself clear?"

"Yes, Madame."

"No, I'm not Madame. I'm Lalla, to be more exact, your Lalla, your mistress, the one who has the right to your life or death."

"Yes, Lalla."

Nabou began working and stopped herself from crying. She told herself never would her man, who was no longer her man, leave her in such conditions. Perhaps she was kidding herself. When Amir returned, his wife informed him about the steps she had taken. He said nothing, and what was the worse, he didn't go to see Nabou. But she didn't see any cowardice in this, and she thought it was his tactic. Only Karim went to see her. His deep sensitivity, his innate kindness, and his intuition made it possible for him to find the words to console her. He promised to get her out of this dark kitchen:

"Karim loves you very much; Karim not possible to leave you in prison . . ."

Nobody had the right to scold Karim. His mother just asked him not to waste his time and to go to take typing lessons. He obeyed her and said: "Mamouche, I love you."

One of the maidservants was Zhora and the other Tam. They came from the same village. Their parents brought them to this family. Once a year, the parents came to see Amir, who gave them some money. The two women didn't know how to read or write and had to work without a single day off. They ate the leftovers and never complained. Nabou didn't know how to communicate with them. They made gestures, exchanged looks, and used a few words in Arabic that Nabou had learned from Amir. There was no sign of outrage in their eyes. Resigned, submissive, they lived on in this big house where the masters prayed, fasted during Ramadan, and even gave alms and went to Mecca for hajj without understanding that their behavior was audacious and went against Islam's principles. But that's how things were. At that time, everybody had maidservants brought from villages and felt no guilt in treating them like slaves.

Only Karim reacted from time to time, especially when Batoule cooked some small dishes just for him that made him very happy. With his limited means of expression, he lamented. One day his father tried to explain this situation to him:

"You see, these poor people were born in the countryside. When there's a bad drought or a poor harvest, they come to the city to find any kind of work. Thus, we help each other. On one hand, Zhora and Tam do the cleaning, wash our clothes, and iron them. We, in return, house and feed them, and once a year I give their parents some money. So everybody wins. If we let them go, they will be even unhappier. This is how the world is. God created different kinds of people—big, small, good and bad, poor, rich . . . We humans can do nothing. That's life."

One day, Karim seemed particularly upset. Making large gestures, he indicated the food and the kitchen where the maids slept. Amir could understand his anger and knew he was right.

"From now on, they will eat the same dishes and not the leftovers. I'll ask Batoule to cook for everyone and serve us all at the same time. The leftovers will be for the cats, ours and those of the neighbors."

Amir didn't do anything about it, though. The words were just to calm an indignant angel.

As for Nabou, Amir knew he would have to take gradual steps. Nothing precipitated, no improvisation, no anger. He felt like being with her more and more. Whenever he thought about her, his heart beat faster; he felt excited and troubled at the same time. All this still felt new to him. When he made love to his white wife, it was Nabou's body that he imagined. He was obsessed by her and dreamed about her all the time. Lalla Fatma could sense it. One evening, she pushed him so hard that he fell off the bed. Her anger was brutal. But they needed to keep up appearances. She refused to make love to him for fifteen nights. Amir was miserable. He couldn't see Nabou because she slept with the servants. It was out of the question to go into the kitchen, as men didn't go there. What could he do? Unless he decided to abuse poor defenseless women while they slept. He had to find a way to give Nabou her own space, not necessarily the guestroom, but at least a room where she would be in peace and he could join her.

Negotiate with Lalla Fatma? Difficult. Making changes and forcing Lalla Fatma to comply? It wasn't that simple. He decided to ask the advice of Moulay Ahmad, whose office was at the Université Al Quaraouiyine.

His counsel carried weight, and no one doubted his competence:

"The marriage."

"A *mut'ah* marriage?"

"No, you are no longer traveling. She is here with you, and, from what you have told me, she is not going back to Africa. You need to solve this in accord with our religion. Turning her into a sex slave or a servant is out of the question. She was your wife for several months. You brought her over here: you owe her respect, you have duties toward her, and you must give her rights. God is merciful, but one has to be just."

"And Lalla Fatma?"

"Since when do women decide in our society? You must regularize the question right away. Don't stay in the '*haram**,' in the sin. God allows a man to have up to four wives on condition, let me repeat, on condition that he loves and treats them equally, e-qui-ta-bly . . . Will you be capable of doing so?"

"I will try."

In principle, it was impossible to reconcile the ways that polygamy was instituted with how it had to be practiced. No man is capable of having the same feelings for four women. In fact, fairness is not attainable. The equity we are talking about is a form of justice. Unable to be fair to the four women, it becomes necessary for him to care for only one. The Islamic law will thus be respected. But all men disregard it and pray that God will pardon them!

Leaving Al Quaraouiyine, Amir felt lighter and decided to marry Nabou. Now it was a matter of how to announce it to Lalla Fatma.

Amir went into Moulay Idriss Mosque, made his ablutions, then, after the midday prayer, he leaned against one of the pillars and stared at the immense chandelier in which some of the bulbs were dead. He dozed off and dreamed he was walking alone in the desert until the moment when a caravan man helped him and took him to a seaport. Then he got on an abandoned ship that had no sailors or a captain, but it drifted by the waves' whims toward a horizon that was sometimes green and red because of the flames rising to the sky. They left behind black smoke that traced enigmatic and disturbing figures. He didn't dare rise, and he allowed himself to be lulled by the shadows. He entered a silent world. He was persuaded that menaces would come with the approaching night as the sky began to merge with the uncertain horizon.

He was not sleeping deeply and could hear around him the noise of the craftsmen and water sellers, as well as the songs of birds lost in this huge mosque's mysteries.

A hand shook him. He woke up and excused himself; it was time for the afternoon prayer. He did like the others, got up and followed the imam, who had a beautiful voice.

Returning home he felt like telling Lalla Fatma about his dream, but he saw that she wasn't in the mood to listen, and she was even less ready to learn about the decision he had made. Often, when he was overwhelmed with too many doubts or worries, he went to see Karim, who always had a way of calming him. He smiled most of the time, made everything seem less alarming, and pointed his index finger to the sky and said: God! This was enough to calm his nerves and push away the worries.

He noticed Nabou. She was doing housework; he watched her for a moment, and, closing his eyes, he remembered the first time she gave herself to him. His decision to officially and legally make her his second wife was final and nothing would change his mind, not even Lalla Fatma's threats. He waited until after his bath on Friday to see his four children and give them the news without offering any explanations. Only Karim applauded. His older brother made a sign for him to stop. There was no discussion.

What remained was the most difficult, to announce it to the white wife. He didn't have to though. Probably informed by one of the children, she herself broached the subject:

"You have brought into this house misfortune, sin, and discord. You want to marry a servant, a Negress whose skin color betrays the blackness of her soul, but does she have a soul? I wonder. Well, you are disappointing. Do what you want. I will take care of my children's education and keep them away from this evil, foul-smelling thing. You are neither the first nor the last to jeopardize a whole family because of a Negress who is allied with Satan. God is great!"

The essential things were said. Amir didn't respond to anything, changed his djellaba*, and left. He would have liked to announce the news to Nabou, but it was not the right moment. He needed to walk in the streets of Fez and reflect on his life's new arrangements. In a narrow alley, a loaded donkey jostled him. He nearly fell, but a hand reached out and helped him regain his balance. He had to fight against the weakness of his character, harden his heart and tone, and become strict, without pity, without regret. He wondered how he was going to do it. How did others do it? He remembered Moulay Ahmad's advice and nodded his head. Yes, I am a man, a good Muslim, and as a Muslim man, I have the right to marry a second woman. I'll stick to my decision. I have feelings for Nabou, and it's the first time I feel this way. I'm in love. With Lalla Fatma, everything was foreseen, planned, no surprises, especially no fantasy. I know I should not talk about feelings and love, as people would make fun of me. These are things that one does not talk about. I never heard my parents say "I love you," and I never saw them kiss or show tenderness to each other. They probably loved each other, but very discreetly, in the strictest privacy. And I, I claim to be in love! I have no one to confide in. "In love," it's not said. Men talk about the body, but rarely about feelings.

He felt like shouting out his love at the Achabine Square, but he stopped himself for fear of people's reaction. Amir was a respected man. He was the very symbol of order and respected dogma. If he shouted that he was in love, people would say that he had lost his mind.

When he returned home, he found out that Lalla Fatma had left for her parents' house. There was no question of going to get her back. The tradition was for the father to bring his daughter back to the conjugal home. That's what happened a few days later. Looking pale and tired, she walked with difficulty and locked herself up immediately in the bedroom. This was her typical way. Silence and tears were her best refuge. She would eventually accept things and be in harmony with the way life was set up by the ancestors, by Islam, and especially by time, which in this city didn't move, but remained frozen in the ninth century.

Amir went back to see Moulay Ahmad. He needed his support and advice. The man was astonished by his lack of courage.

"Be a man, be strong and don't let yourself be swayed by the craftiness of women. As Islam says, 'Their capacity for making things difficult is infinite.' So, do what you have to do and don't remain in this shaky and hesitating state, because you are lucky to have the physical condition and material means to satisfy four women. Don't have any more hesitation. Marry the Black and live in peace."

When he came back home, Amir gathered his four children again: Mohamed, the eldest, Aziz, Fatiha, and Karim, and he explained to them his intentions more clearly:

"As I told you the other day, I've decided to marry Nabou, the young woman who has come here with me from Africa. She's a good person who makes me happy. Under no circumstances is this marriage intended to hurt your mother. Our religion is like this, and I cannot live in sin. I have already contracted with this woman a temporary marriage. Today, she lives with us, and I will make her my second wife according to the law and the Sunna* of our Prophet, may God's salvation be upon him. I wanted to inform you all. As for the rest, nothing will change."

Silence. Not a word, no reaction. They got up and left one after another. Only Karim came to kiss his father.

The other three children went to see their mother to show her their support. Mohamed spoke on behalf of the others:

"Mother, know that we love you, and you can count on us. If Father has committed an error, a sin, God will put him back on the right path. This new wife must stay far from our house. We are united and in solidarity with you."

Amir suspected his children would behave this way despite their lack of reaction in front of him.

On the following Friday, two *adouls**, men of religion, notaries of sorts, arrived at the house where Amir, dressed all in white, was waiting for them. They had to write on the certificate in which Lalla Fatma's name was written the new marriage with Nabou, born in Thiès, Senegal. The ceremony was brief. Nabou, who was also dressed in white, put her signature on the marriage certificate, and a dowry of fabrics and some gold jewelry was given to her. A prayer was said. A heavy silence reigned in the courtyard where the little stream of water from a fountain in the middle made the sound of a bird.

The first wedding night was quiet. The tensions of the last few weeks had exhausted them, and neither was able to make love as they were used to during their *mut'ah* marriage. They fell asleep holding each other. Nabou cried a little, perhaps out of joy, perhaps fatigue. In the early morning, Amir felt a strong desire rise in him. His erection couldn't leave Nabou indifferent and they finally made love.

In Fez there were two kinds of people: the Fassis, whose ancestors came from Arabia or Andalusia, and the others. These others did not exist. One had no respect for them. Nabou had no chance of finding her place in this city and even less in the big house. One day, Amir had a dizzy spell. Nabou experienced a moment of panic: What would be her fate if, unfortunately, he passed away? This made her reflect. No doubt she would be immediately thrown into the street without anything, not even her own belongings. She felt a twinge in her heart and prayed silently that God may preserve her husband and offer him good health.

At the hammam, she met a black masseuse who had been brought back from Guinea, and who had found herself out in the street the day after her master died. He used to protect her, but hadn't married her. This woman had lost everything. She didn't know what her name was, how she had arrived in this city, or how she had gotten this painful and poorly paid job. She stammered, but Nabou understood the important things she said. There was no law in force that defended such people. Officially, there was no slavery, but people practiced it without scruple. It was the order of things.

The masseuse slept in a small room in the hallway of the hammam. She was given food from time to time. When she didn't work, she begged at the entrance of the mausoleum of Moulay Idriss, patron saint of the city. Nabou understood her situation, and, whenever possible, she gave the masseuse some money.

Even though she was married, Nabou had no guarantee, no security for her future. She didn't dare to talk about this with Amir, who downplayed everything. So she decided to give him a child. She did her calculations and achieved her ends. Three months after their marriage, Nabou was pregnant.

This news had a devastating effect on Lalla Fatma, who suffered a kind of paralysis on the left side. Disfigured, unable to get up or scream, she shut herself in the bedroom and once again refused to receive her husband. Only the children could see her. Karim, very affected by her condition, made efforts to say how much he loved her and even to make her laugh. Far from everything, trapped in her anxieties, feeling humiliated, she lost weight and refused to take her medicine. Her parents often came to visit her, especially to explain that it was in her interest to accept the fact of the new wife. She cried and repeated: "Never, never in my life will I accept being replaced by a Negress, a dirty foreigner who doesn't even know how to speak. She has bewitched my husband, she has cast a spell on him, and I, too, am her victim. These are savage people who hate us because God has made us white and clean and they are human waste."

Her father asked her to come to her senses and not to say such absurd things that were unworthy of a Muslim. He read verses from the Koran to calm her, but her hatred and bitterness were stronger than everything else.

The house was far from being a haven of peace. Amir had his meals with Nabou; the children served themselves in the kitchen, and their mother didn't leave her room. There was no longer any family life. The one who suffered the most was Karim. His condition deteriorated a little, and even the typewriter didn't interest him anymore. The servants were confused and nothing worked as before. Nabou, to be on the safe side, didn't get involved. The youngest of the servants was placed at her service. She accompanied her once a week to the hammam. There was always the masseuse, who took very good care of her.

All of Amir's attempts to reconcile with Lalla Fatma were unsuccessful. Moulay Ahmad advised him to wait. One day she would wake up and forget all her negative thoughts.

Every year Amir organized a great mystical evening on the eve of the twenty-seventh night of Ramadan. He invited the entire family, friends, tolbas*, readers of the Koran, and Sufi poets. The children loved this long night when they went up to the rooftop to look at the stars, persuaded that everyone had their own star and that it shone more brightly than the others.

Lalla Fatma could not stay locked in her room and not participate as usual at this reception. She decided to come out and greet the guests as she usually did. Her paralysis had almost disappeared. She had returned to her normal appearance. Had peace come back? She stood next to her husband. Nabou stood a little farther, pregnant and smiling. At a certain moment, everyone went to the Moulay Idriss mausoleum for the dawn prayer. As during all festivities, the children played and didn't sleep. The men walked ahead and the women followed them. The procession entered the mausoleum. The women settled in the back rows, the men in the front, and the prayers were said aloud. At sunrise, everyone left the mosque. Amir accompanied Lalla Fatma to their bedroom. They slept together without touching each other. In any case, it was forbidden while fasting. But something had brought peace to the couple.

Apparently calm, Lalla Fatma was not prepared to make peace with Nabou. A few weeks after the end of Ramadan, she sent for a shaggy, badly dressed guy who trailed a cardboard suitcase behind him. He went straight to the kitchen and asked to be fed raw meat, claiming he needed it for his work. Batoule obeyed him and wasn't at all impressed by this guy, who was clearly a charlatan. But she had seen others like him and knew her mistress believed in this kind of practice, which led to nothing but spending her husband's money unnecessarily.

After devouring everything that was given to him, he burped loudly and drank a large bowl of hot water. He then shut himself up in Lalla Fatma's room, and no one knew what he was doing there.

This wizard was going to drive Nabou away and, most importantly, provoke a miscarriage. Lalla Fatma's greatest fear was the risk that a black child who would bear the same name as her own children would be born in the family. This idea made her mad with rage. She said:

"That he has been having fun with a whore, I can take it, but that he will have children with her, it's unbearable. She must croak before."

The wizard told Lalla Fatma that he needed a lock of Nabou's hair and also some of her pubic hair. Difficult task. How to succeed in getting it so that the witchcraft could work? She could have one of the servants cut some hair during Nabou's sleep, but the pubic hair, only Amir could provide it. How can one imagine making him an accomplice? He was in love with this woman and would never let anyone hurt her. While she was thinking aloud, she had an idea: bribe the masseuse at the hammam who could shave her during the massage. She feared solidarity between the two Blacks, but she decided to try anyway, thinking that money could cause miracles.

The negotiation with the masseuse was difficult. She couldn't understand what Lalla Fatma was asking for. Another masseuse, a White, proposed to pull off Nabou's pubic hair for a good sum of money.

Fifteen days later, Lalla Fatma had the two kinds of hair. She hid them in a safe place and waited for the return of the wizard, who was going around the city and stayed for a day or two in Meknes to heal a child who had suddenly lost his sight.

Nabou could sense that Lalla Fatma was planning some bad trick. But she felt protected by the spirit of her ancestors. Nothing bad could happen to her. In addition, since she was Muslim, she confided in God and claimed his beneficence and his mercy. She had learned Arabic to pray and recite some verses from the Koran. She mixed French and Arabic, but what mattered was her intention to be on the right path of God. Her belly was getting bigger, which made her look even more beautiful. When she moved, she seemed light and walked on tiptoe. Amir liked spoiling her and kissed her belly when he arrived at home or before he left. He felt like a young man, in love and happy. Even though business was not going well because of political unrest, he didn't complain like his neighbors and cousins. Business was not his priority. He was obsessed by this pregnancy, counted the days, and didn't hide his impatience. He contacted Touria, the midwife, but she had aged and was not working anymore. It was Kenza, her niece and a nurse at the French hospital, who replaced her. She came to examine Nabou and announced confidently:

"It will be in ten days. They are twins."

Amir almost lost his balance. Nabou laughed nervously. Two Blacks in the family! It would be enough to finish Lalla Fatma.

In this city without horizon, where the houses are built close to each other and the alleys weave a cramped labyrinth, where life seems written in advance in a large notebook placed on the tomb of the city's patron saint, everyone has to stay in their place. In no case should women go beyond the borders set down by men over the centuries; the poor must be satisfied with their status as poor, and those who are rich should continue doing business and not look back or feel a sense of injustice. They have to give alms, treat the poor kindly, and thank God for lavishing them with so many possessions.

Amir was plunged in these reflections when Karim flung himself into his arms as though he was desperate for affection. He wanted to cry. The schoolmaster had sent him home because he couldn't pronounce the word "spectacle," which he pronounced as "pistale." Amir had noticed that Karim often regressed when something was bothering him.

"What's going on, my son?"

"I'm scared . . ."

"Scared of what?

"Maman sick, Maman cries, cries . . ."

"Don't worry about it. You're going to have a new baby brother or a sister."

"I know, Nabou is pre . . . pre . . . nent . . . having baby."

"That's right. From now on, I'm counting on you to help me at the store. The rest of the time, a teacher will come home to give you lessons. He won't make you cry like the other imbecile."

"A teacher for me alone?"

"Meanwhile, you'll go to the store with me. I need to put things in order."

Karim liked being given responsibilities. Working with his father would be better than having therapy. A nurse had told Amir that a speech therapist had just moved into the new town. Amir checked and confirmed that, indeed, the specialist was opening an office in the French neighborhood. He wrote down his name and address and told Karim that he would be seeing a new doctor. Karim said with a big smile:

"Not si . . . sick, me!"

His new teacher turned out to be Moulay Ahmad's youngest son. He spent two hours every day teaching Karim to read and write.

Nabou was given a beautiful room that was very similar to that of Lalla Fatma. She continued being discreet. The two women didn't speak to each other. Amir spent two nights a week with the white wife, who still refused to make love to him. Even pregnant, Nabou caressed Amir and offered him great tenderness. When their mother informed her sons about Nabou's pregnancy, they were embarrassed; only the daughter took a clear position against the black woman and let it be known by shouting:

"If I were to get married someday, I'd marry a Christian, a foreigner from a country where polygamy is forbidden, where Blacks don't mix with Whites. Father doesn't know what he's doing anymore; he is not himself anymore, and he is under the evil influence of a tribe. You'll see, one day they will all come here and invade us, take all that belongs to us, and throw us out!"

Lalla Fatma, who never left her room, saw through the window how Kenza was bustling around. Nabou was about to give birth. Lalla Fatma watched this bustle and couldn't stop a teardrop from rolling down. She was sad and, at the same time, wanted to make an effort to accept the situation and get used to it. But she wasn't ready. She felt as though she had lost her husband. She felt as if she were dead and witnessing her husband's new life with this black woman, who made him happy. She asked herself questions about their behavior, about their sexuality, and cursed African women. She didn't feel she was being racist. In any case, Moroccans always considered others to be racists. Where did this stupid idea that Blacks have a particularly powerful sexuality come from?

Amir was at home. Karim was taking care of the store. The servants were busy cleaning the house. Batoule got some lamb offal to make a soup to give strength to the young mother after childbirth. Everything was ready to welcome the newborn or newborns.

Amir stayed at a distance, telling his prayer beads. Lalla Fatma swallowed a capsule, was served her herbal tea, and fell asleep. It was out of the question for her to take part in this event that had been hurting her so much. Her daughter did the same thing; she set up a mattress in her mother's room, next to her, and decided to sleep during the delivery.

When the first baby was born, Batoule gave out a strident ululation that woke up her mistress. At the birth of the second, she shouted: "Allah Akbar!" Kenza was dumbstruck. As she had anticipated, they were certainly twins, but one of them was black, very black and reddish. In fact, one was darker than the other, but it was only a few days later when it became evident that the first was white, very white, the second black, totally black.

Kenza had never seen anything like this, not even imagined such a thing could be possible. She said:

"It's a sign from God! A blessing, a double gain."

Amir, greatly filled with emotion, simply said:

"Hassan and Hussein.* I'll call them Hassan and Hussein. It's the tradition."

He once again consulted Moulay Ahmad on this phenomenon. "Normally, your children should be café au lait color; you have one that's black coffee, the other, with milk. God has his reasons. Accept this gift of God and tell yourself it is a sign of his beneficence. God has created diversity in humanity so that people accept and help each other. He does not make any difference between those who are from here and those from elsewhere. That's how it is. Consider yourself privileged; you are lucky and don't waste this luck on useless things. Give them a good education in our faith and our religion."

Karim couldn't hide his joy at having two new little brothers. He sang and danced like the time when he won a swimming competition. He missed his morning training session so he could be home for the delivery. It was he who announced the news to his mother, who didn't show any surprise. She even said:

"Here's proof that she's a witch. One is white and the other black! Nobody ever saw this before."

Karim didn't tell anyone about this comment. He ran into the house to announce the news to everyone. He got himself a saucepan and started beating it with a wooden spoon:

"Announcement to ev . . . ev . . . everybody! Hass . . . Hassan and Huss . . . Hussein are here . . . Long live Papa, long live Maman . . ."

He was stopped by his elder brother, who reminded him that Nabou wasn't his mother.

"Yes, I know, but Nabou is mother of Hassan and Huss . . . Hussein . . . my brothers!"

On the seventh day after the birth, Amir had two sheep sacrificed and named his two sons. Moulay Ahmad raised his clasped hands and asked all the men attending the ceremony to pray with him, asking Almighty God: "May these two children be welcome in this world, may they be blessed by God, and may they proclaim goodness, prosperity, serenity, and peace in the religion of Allah and his Messenger, Sidna Muhammad; may they be guided on the right path of our faith and our values that make us mere passengers in this life and remember that we belong to God and we will return to him according to his sacred will . . ."

After the prayer, lunch was a feast. All that was missing were the musicians whom Amir had dared not call lest he provoke Lalla Fatma's jealousy.

But hurt and angry, she couldn't take it any longer.

A few days later, she sent Batoule to fetch the wizard, who had been ill and was no longer going around. So she decided to go see him herself. For that, she needed her husband's authorization. She invented a story about the Jewish upholsterer who had to redo the living room, but who, due to health reasons, didn't go out of the Mellah anymore. So she said to Amir:

"If you let me, I'll go to see him and give the measurements of the mattresses that need to be made again. Give me some money in advance. Also, I feel like going out, seeing other people; I need a change of air."

She put on her gray djellaba and her small white veil that hid her mouth and chin. Then she left the medina with Batoule to find the wizard, who waited for them at the entrance of a warehouse.

"Do you have what I asked for?"

She gave him the lock of Nabou's hair and the pubic hair that she had kept in a handkerchief.

"You should have come earlier; the entire town is talking about the twins, one black, the other white. Now what can we do?"

She gave him some banknotes and said:

"It's your problem. The goal is for this woman to return to where she came from, and, of course, with the one she has slept with."

The wizard gave her a talisman that she would have to slide under Nabou's bed.

"As a result, she will lose her sleep. Then she will lose her mind—you'll see that she will leave the house in a fury. But I'll do something for a more efficient and quick reaction. I'll need some gold threads to tie the talismans with. You can give them to Batoule."

In the evening, Amir asked Lalla Fatma about the upholsterer.

"I couldn't find him; I was told he has been hospitalized."

"That's interesting, because this afternoon he came to get paid for the work he did before I went to Africa. He was in good health. You're hiding something from me."

She mumbled a few words and then went off to her room. Amir advised Nabou to pay attention to what Batoule gave her to eat. He knew what a jealous woman was capable of.

Over time, Amir understood that he should not have Nabou live in the same house as his white wife. He had to find another house in the neighborhood, where he could move her away from the danger that threatened her. But he couldn't afford it. He summoned the cook and warned her against any witchcraft to which his young wife might fall victim. He made her swear on the Koran that she would never harm Nabou. He was not afraid of scribbles and talismans, but was afraid of substances like the brain of the hyena, which, mixed with food, could cause paralysis and behavioral problems. She promised never to harm Nabou, yet she would pretend to obey her mistress so as not to provoke Lalla Fatma's wrath. Batoule didn't like that her mistress made her work unceasingly.

One day, Amir decided to rent a dishwasher that a company in the new town had imported from France. After a month, if he liked it, he could buy it at a good price. He would be the first Fassi man to install this machine at his place. He felt proud to make the servants' work easier. They were fascinated and overjoyed; it was like a dream for them. No more washing chores. A technician explained the machine's operation and gave them some advice before leaving. They were amazed and wondered if it would displease their mistress. Without giving a long speech, Lalla Fatma, out of pure meanness, forbade them to use it:

"You have hands and arms; tell my husband that you don't need this machine, which is good for the handicapped, for the lazy, and not for you. So, he will have to return it. The first one who touches it will regret it for the rest of her life. Understood?"

Two men came to take it away. The servants watched as the machine disappeared. They had tears in their eyes. The mistress's words hurt them. But they were used to being treated like slaves. They knew that someday justice would be done. They dared not speak about it with Amir. In any case, they didn't have the right to speak to him. He obeyed his wife to avoid a new drama. It wasn't the moment to annoy her.

Amir continued to spend two nights with his white wife, who, after a while, agreed to resume sexual relations with him. The tepidness of these moments made him sad and bitter. They fulfilled a conjugal duty, without pleasure, without joy, without fantasy. He was much happier sleeping with Nabou, who, despite having just given birth, hadn't lost her sensuality and prowess. Her breasts had grown bigger and Amir sucked them like the babies while caressing her body that had become even more exciting and smoother.

The wizard's work had no effect on Nabou or her children. Lalla Fatma ended up accepting the situation and decided to wait for the right moment to take revenge.

The engagement party of Amir's only daughter, Fatiha, took place in a tense atmosphere and was nearly ruined. Hassan and Hussein were two years old; they ran around like little devils in the big house. The fiancé's mother asked where the black child came from. Amir replied in a firm and somewhat threatening tone:

"He's my son, Hassan, Hussein's twin brother, and the fiancée's half brother."

Silence. Sidelong glances. The two *adouls* who had to register the act were asking what they should do. Lalla Fatma intervened:

"He is just Fatiha's half brother. Let's not make a big deal out of such a small thing. It just smells like a greasy knife blade, nothing more."

"Yes, but he is black!" said the future fiancé's father. "We are going to join our family with one in which one of the fiancée's brothers is black. It's not in our traditions. How do we know that Fatiha will not give birth to a Black?"

"So what?" cried Amir. "I wanted to name him Bilal, like the black slave freed by our Prophet, but since he has a twin brother, I decided upon Hassan and Hussein. What harm do you see in that? And also, skin color is not contagious!"

Pin-drop silence. Karim managed to lighten the atmosphere by playing a lively rhythm on the piano. Everybody clapped. He had reason to be happy; he had saved the situation.

The two *adouls* had the good idea to recite the sura Fatiha right then and raise their joined hands so that God would bless this union and make peace and serenity reign in their hearts. Uncle Brahim offered the couple twelve silver spoons. There was a superstition that buying spoons for oneself brought bad luck.

Around that time, a rumor was spread by the hammam cashier, who accused Nabou of stealing Hussein, the white child. It went around the medina quickly, and it reached Amir. As he was preparing to close the store, a jealous and mean-spirited neighbor approached him and muttered into his ear:

"That you fuck a hot Black, it's okay, but allowing her to make you believe that she's the mother of the white child is gross!"

Amir didn't respond, lowered his head, and went home.

Lalla Fatma immediately asked the question:

"Were you in the room when she gave birth? I guess not, so the white baby could have been stolen with the help of the new midwife—a pervert, a debauchee, and an unmarried woman whose bed is full of men. Her testimony is worthless. Don't bother asking her to come here and tell us lies."

For the first time in his life, Amir was carried away by a moment of rare violence.

He screamed with all his force:

"I will no longer tolerate this war you're fighting against Lalla Nabou. And yes, she's a princess, a woman of high class, dignified and magnificent. So that's enough, yes, that's enough! I don't want to hear another word against her anymore. To attack her is to attack my honor, my integrity, and me. So, you stop!"

She dared ask:

"If not?"

"If not, repudiation! It'll take one minute, the time to write the letter to return you and for you to pack your bags. It's enough if I pronounce three times in a row, 'You are repudiated,' for you to stop being my wife. That's the law!"

Lalla Fatma burst out crying, because she knew he wasn't joking, and she disappeared into her room. She had never seen her husband in such a state. For her, it was the result of African witchcraft.

Nabou was informed by one of the servants who had overheard the argument between Amir and his wife. Nothing surprised her anymore, but she began to fear that someone might come and take her children away. She knew that everything was possible in this city, that treacherous schemes were many and everywhere. She slept holding both children in her arms. Amir took advantage of their birthday to mark the occasion and put an end to this horrible rumor. He went around, Hassan on one side and Hussein on the other, followed by their mother, who had dressed that day in one of her beautiful African dresses. Lalla Fatma sulked in her room; she felt as though she were witnessing her own end, and she began to give up her prayers, claiming that God had preferred a black woman over her.

The watchword "Mohammed V is in the moon" spread very quickly throughout the city one day in November 1955. All Moroccans were given an opportunity to see the appearance of their king on the moon's face. It had been a nice day, the sky was filled with stars, and the Moroccan people went up to their rooftops, the hills, the trees, and a few buildings to see the apparition on the moon, the profile of the one whom France had removed and exiled with his family very far from his country, in Madagascar. It was rare that such a phenomenon was as enthusiastically followed with so much conviction by the masses. It was not their imagination. Some said they saw him smiling, others claimed he looked calm and confident, that his return to the throne was inevitable, and that it was only a matter of weeks. Politicians would soon find a way that could not only bring the ruler back to his palace, but also give independence to Morocco. After all, this protectorate had lasted long enough, and, besides, France was fighting a terrible war in Algeria that would hurt both peoples and leave irreparable wounds.

Nobody dared joke about this surreal apparition, not even Amir's cousin, Hafid, a former clandestine anarchist and anti-monarchist teacher who was threatened with death by nationalist militants. He was hiding, and, whenever he could, he shouted his passion for the French Revolution of 1789. Amir had shown him a shack where he could hide. From time to time, he sent Hafid some food, and he went to him only at night, hiding himself in an old djellaba:

"Listen, Hafid, stop playing the provocateur. You are going against Morocco's current direction because all the Moroccans love their king and are fighting for his return. So stop acting like a fool."

"Yes, but what has this monarchy done for the well-being of the citizens?"

Hafid had suffered, and he was not like other people. He was one of the children of the black slave whom his father had brought back from Guinea. He was métis. Despised, humiliated, he had quickly learned that no one would be nice to him, so he began to read day and night and set up a library for himself. The books had allowed him to finally find his identity, a sense of balance and calm. Racism was almost natural in a society that had always rejected and treated people with black skin as inferior. He had read Voltaire and Hugo, Zola and Rabelais, Rimbaud and Omar Khayyam, Khalil Gibran and André Gide, Ahmed Shawqi and Anatole France, Georges Darien and Taha Hussein. He devoured everything that came to hand, took notes, and memorized some excerpts.

Hafid used to say to his uncle:

"I am self-made; my father abandoned me. Luckily, I found all these books at the flea market. They belonged to the French who left Morocco at the moment of political events."

Hafid loved reading novels. He was often a passionate reader. However, some readings could turn into obsession. He had a hard time freeing himself from Kafka's *Metamorphosis*. Every morning, he rushed to the mirror to make sure he had not physically transformed during the night. One day he noticed a wart under the left side of his lips. The next day, it had moved and even gotten bigger. He opened the pocket edition of Kafka's book, and he got frightened. There were no words on the pages; instead, there were drawings caricaturing his face with a dozen warts of different sizes. He even heard a voice saying that he would from then on find his destiny written on these pages. He began to panic. He attributed these troubles to fatigue. Yet nothing oppressed him: no overwork, because his job as an unofficial tourist guide was quite calm. But something was bothering him and he couldn't identify it. When he bent over to take his long pipe and stuff it with kif*, he realized that it was this grass that was playing tricks on him. He put it away and drank a big glass of water. He had always smoked, but for the first time he felt that the kif was causing these hallucinations.

When he took up Kafka's novel again, after a long nap, there was nothing abnormal about the book. Nothing was erased and there were no drawings. He looked at himself in the mirror and smiled as if to say, "Stop your bullshit."

The cover of *The Gods Are Thirsty* by Anatole France was white and thick. His friend José had offered him this novel and told him to read it as soon as possible: "How lucky you are to discover this masterpiece for the first time!"

He plunged into the reading. He felt as though he could hear the voice of revolt. He was delighted. It was the kind of literature he liked the most. In his dreams, he saw his father on a donkey, lost in the heat of a deserted village and shouting: "I forgive God for giving me a miserable son who respects nothing and makes revolt his only religion; this has nothing to do with our history—we are loyal monarchists, and we do not want to cut off anyone's head! May God forgive him!" He said to himself that no one would make his father pay for anything, that one had almost a religious relationship with the parents. One accepted them as they were and never disrespected them. Otherwise, it would mean a breakup with them and public rejection.

Hafid was a rebel, but not a bad son; he could not blame his father, who had abandoned him. As for his mother, she disappeared after being sold to a wealthy landowner in the Meknes region.

One day Hafid explained to his uncle and benefactor, Amir, his point of view without raising his voice: "The French should never have deposed the king, and if they had left him in place, the monarchy would have died by itself. Now, by turning him into a hero, and Mohammed V is a hero, they have condemned Morocco to perpetuate the monarchical system and strengthened it. The proof—all the people are in the street claiming his return to the throne of his ancestors! I personally have nothing against this family, but, frankly, how long do we have to pledge our allegiance to a king and remain his submissive subjects? I may be the only one to think this way. But I'm telling you what I think, my friend, my uncle. I know I'll be lynched if I speak up. So, I'm going away. Sorry!" Amir tried to tell him that the republican systems were not necessarily democracies; he pointed to the example of Egypt, where Nasser had just taken power through a military coup. Amir told him, being a cautious man, how much this country needed stability, and that the king as commander of the believers was the only one capable of uniting the Moroccans under the banner of a peaceful Islam.

Hafid knew that his position was that of the ultra-minority, but he continued being stubborn. He had stopped working as a guide, especially because the authorities had set up a militia against unofficial guides. His decision was made: self-exile. He had looked into several countries, and his choice was made: Sweden. He said it was his dream, his ambition. Why this country? It's because at that time Sweden had just adopted several hundred orphaned children after a civil war in an African country. The press had talked a lot about it, and Hafid felt himself to be both an orphan and an African! In addition, he had studied about the political systems of the Nordic countries.

But he didn't have a passport and was counting on Amir to get him one. It was going to be difficult. Those who delivered them were mostly Algerian officials with French status. There were many of them working in the police and intelligence. The nationalists avoided them and did not hide their disapproval. Fatiha's future husband knew someone who worked secretly for the French police. Amir approached him seeking to have a passport issued to Hafid, who was born to a Moroccan father and a Guinean mother. With an envelope slipped into the file among all the documents requested by the man, Hafid obtained his passport and, without informing anyone except Amir—who had given him money—filled a suitcase with books, took the boat to Tangier, then the train to Algeciras up to Stockholm, which he discovered on a December evening completely covered with snow.

He had never before seen this thing that was depicted in the novels. It was strange and quite euphoric. Like a child, he made snowballs and pressed them to his face. He was so happy to walk on the soil of this dream country that he didn't feel the cold. He knew somebody there, a countryman who had come to this country with a much older female tourist. Hafid was well received. It was again necessary to fill out forms, talk a little about his life, the reasons behind the exile, etc. His friend told him about an important fact: "Here, we don't lie, no need to dramatize your situation; here a White is equal to a Black or a métis, which is your case, right? The Nordics are honest; they are not Mediterranean, no excessive gestures, no familiarity; you have the same rights as all the other citizens. You must start by learning the language and then look for a job. The important thing is to be serious and get straight to the point. No politics, I mean, forget your hostility toward the Moroccan monarchy. It doesn't interest them. If you conduct yourself correctly, you will get everything the law allows, but at the least negative action, you'll be sent home without any warning. But I know you're smart, and you'll succeed. Forget your anarchist and slightly deluded ideas, okay?"

"Okay! You can count on me. I have only one religion: seriousness, rigor, and what is right!"

A few months later he sent his benefactor Amir a photo in which he was posing in the arms of a pretty blonde, who was taller than him. They were at a ski resort. Amir had this thought: In Morocco, he would never have been in the arms of a white woman and he would never have known skiing! We should send a bouquet of roses to the royal family of Sweden!

Since the twins were born, Amir had become aware of a reality that, until then, he had witnessed only from a distance because it didn't concern him. Racism was widespread in the minds of all, rich and poor, the people of Fez and those of other cities. Yet the Moroccan population was not entirely white. There were, of course, descendants of slaves, who lived mostly in the south and worked menial jobs. The most meritorious among them were chosen to be part of the royal guard. The king had given an order that this particular guard be composed only of Blacks, striking proof of an almost unconscious racism that didn't offend anyone apart from its victims. But nobody seemed to care; no one reacted to this situation in a Morocco that was still under the protectorate, on the eve of independence.

After Fatiha's marriage, Mohamed, Amir's eldest son, and also Aziz, went to study in Cairo after obtaining a scholarship from a Muslim association. The father had seen no danger, believing in the goodness of these Muslims who were already active in the shadows. He had no idea he was giving up his children to a political movement that, in Egypt, opposed modernity. Only Karim was left at home; he lovingly took care of his two brothers while spending a lot of time on the typewriter, where, as he said, he kept his "diary." Lalla Fatma became desperate in her corner. As soon as Amir went somewhere, she gave orders that the children of the black woman eat the leftovers from the kitchen, which made Nabou terribly upset. She managed to escape Lalla Fatma to the extent that she avoided and never confronted her.

Amir had more and more difficulties with his business. Frequent strikes and demonstrations kept customers away. He talked about it with Brahim, his older brother who left Fez in the 1940s to settle in Tangier, where he opened several currency exchange counters. After some thinking, he encouraged Amir to join him in the prosperous and flourishing city on the Strait of Gibraltar.

Lalla Fatma died in her sleep one night when a strong storm hit Fez and nearly destroyed everything. They had to wait for the end of the torrential rains to bury her and receive the people who came to offer their condolences. The three days devoted to the funeral seemed endless. It was necessary to feed the people, to lodge them, and to answer those who asked questions about Nabou. "Is this a new servant?" some asked, knowing very well who she was. Others didn't beat around the bush and accused her of precipitating Lalla Fatma's death. All this was wanton nastiness. God had created white human beings. Blacks were the errors of nature that had nothing to do with God's chosen great families, who were well loved by his Prophet. These were the phrases that were being murmured during the days of mourning, which brought all kinds of people together. There was the obese uncle who had an opinion on everything and didn't hesitate to give it. He had a tic and couldn't help picking his nose in public. His wife, known to have a malicious tongue, contented herself with casting hateful glances at the twins and at their mother, who stood quietly in a corner, dressed in white, the mourning color. There was Amir's younger brother, miserly and blunt, who kept talking about the problem of inheritance. He asked:

"What more do we need! Now we have Blacks in a noble family that descended from the Prophet's lineage. We need to be careful, as black women are known to practice witchcraft. It is they who, along with the Jews, have invented what we call 'black magic.' It's normal, these two species are resentful toward us!" A cousin, polygamous and happy to live comfortably with his revenues, proposed to find Amir a young and beautiful woman from Fez, white and pure: "We should not leave him alone with this slave; it seems that these women know sexual tricks that make white men go crazy!" There was also the Koranic schoolmaster, thin and toothless, who always had a hand under the djellaba to hold his penis, whose reactions he could not control. He claimed that once a métis servant had cast a spell on him to the point that he had to move from his neighborhood, and he repeated to those who listened to him that God severely punishes adultery, especially with women of color. And finally, there was Brahim, Amir's eldest brother from Tangier. He was the only one to walk up to Nabou and present his condolences, and he asked her not to worry about the remarks made by these imbeciles. When he left, he reminded her that his house was open to them: "You and your children will always be welcome at my place."

Amir was sorrowful, even though the death of his wife was also a deliverance, and it was the will of God. The order of things was now broken. He had to reorganize his new family life. He responded to everyone at the funeral by means of polite expressions appropriate to the circumstances; he recited a verse on tolerance, recalling that God created diverse and similar human beings, and that the only difference among them was in the force of their faith and in the rigor of their knowledge.

After the ceremony of the fortieth day* following Lalla Fatma's death, Amir decided to go on a trip to Tangier to see if there was any work he could do there and settle in the city with his wife and children. His brother advised him not to waste time and to quickly get his family there. Business seemed to be flourishing, so there was no need to look too closely. A border city, Tangier was no exception to the rule. Here, everything was possible. It was a good epoch for some, bad for those who still held on to their principles and values.

Chapter 5

At the end of the fifties, Tangier, unlike the other big cities of Morocco, enjoyed the particular status of an international city, thanks to the American, English, Italian, French, Spanish, Indian, and German foreign legations that were installed there. It seemed that, since forever, spies and bandits of all kinds met there to play spies and bandits. When things went wrong, the pasha of Tangier, the famous Pasha Tazi, intervened and put order in this anthill that gathered in the two big hotels of the city: the Continental, which overlooked the port, and El Minzah, located a few steps from the French consulate.

The times were prosperous for Brahim, an unscrupulous businessman experienced in trickery, while his brother Amir was more attracted to mysticism than to trade. Brahim had found a niche: the clandestine traffic of goods between Gibraltar and Tangier, which he organized like no one else. To those who looked at him with reproachful eyes, he said: "This city is not made for the law; those who do not know how to lie will never make a fortune here." The fact that Brahim knew how to speak several languages greatly helped his business relations, in which trade and political-Mafia scheming blended together. Brahim could never be fooled; he knew how to please everyone and took great care to report all his schemes to his friend Labbar, an agent of the pasha. This Labbar also had valuable connections with Tangier's Indian traders, an urban group who lived in their own neighborhood, were admired and respected, and didn't mix with the Moroccans. They paid Labbar at the end of each month to have his protection in case of difficulties.

Before leaving on his journey to Tangier to change his life and embark on an adventure he was not prepared for, Amir asked one of his nephews to sell the big house in Fez. It was a difficult time. The real estate market was nonexistent, and everyone advised him against selling this little palace that he had inherited from his parents and grandparents. The weeks passed and no buyers were found. Finally, the nephew offered to buy it himself at a very low price. Amir didn't argue, and he left this house where he had spent so many happy days and decided to forget about it.

Amir arrived in Tangier in the middle of the night. He knew little about the city where he had come only for brief periods to visit his brother. Karim, Nabou, and the twins accompanied him. After a week with Brahim, who lived in a beautiful villa in La Vieille Montagne, they settled in a big, dilapidated house that had the advantage of being built on top of a shop. Amir followed his brother's advice to the letter and began to sell fabric that he bought from a Polish Jew who had fled his country because of antisemitism; in the neighborhood he was called Polako. He found in Tangier peace and fortune that Poland had refused him.

Amir heard the rumor that Polako had fallen in love with his neighbor's wife, a woman from the Rif, whose husband was a sailor. Every day, going to the market or the hammam, she stopped for a short moment in front of the fabric merchant's shop, and then continued on her way. She would have liked to go in and buy a piece of fabric to upholster her living room and chat a little, but she knew everyone was watching her. One day the husband learned from a neighbor that Polako was interested in his wife. Taking a big kitchen knife, he suddenly showed up at his house:

"So, Polako, it seems that you like my wife? Come closer so that I can cut off your dick. We'll see if, after that, you're still checking her out."

Polako had the fear of his life. He mumbled some excuses and vowed not to look up at her again.

"No, you have to move. It's an order, and you have no choice. And hurry up, because I'm expert at cutting dicks . . ."

Polako packed up overnight. It was said that he settled in Casablanca, where, with help from the chief rabbi, he opened a kosher butcher's shop. In the meantime, because of this unfortunate story, Amir and Brahim lost their best supplier, and Amir had to change his business. He was now working with the Indians and selling cameras, Philips transistors, Teppaz record players, and imported Parker pens.

In Tangier, Amir lived far away from his other three children. The boys were studying in Cairo. As for his married daughter, she lived in Oujda and didn't give him any news of herself. They visited him only on the occasion of the celebration of the end of Ramadan and that of the Sacrifice of the Sheep*. They had never accepted the presence of Nabou in their father's life. Only Karim completely accepted her; he had overcome the sorrow caused by his mother's death.

These difficult relations with his older children often made Amir unhappy. It had caused an irremediable melancholy to grow within him. He paid less attention to himself, went to work with less enthusiasm, was sometimes silent, and isolated himself. The presence of Nabou and Karim kept him going, as did the hope of securing a proper future for Hassan and Hussein. So he paid great attention to their studies and comfort.

Nabou was always very tender and supportive. She simplified his daily life and tried to avoid conflicts. In the summer, when Amir's eldest son arrived unexpectedly and loudly claimed the inheritance of property that had belonged to his mother, Nabou calmed him down and managed to get him to leave before his father's return. She advised him to make peace with his father, to go see him and claim his blessing, but he stubbornly refused and made threats against him.

This kind of behavior was completely unacceptable at the time. In no case could a son go after his father. He risked exclusion from the family and even the possibility of being disinherited. This happened very rarely. It happened to Hamza, a rebellious son who collaborated with the French police in denouncing his uncle and his friends who met in an abandoned house to organize resistance against the French presence in Morocco. When the father heard that the traitor was none other than his son, he went to the center of Diwane, cursed him in public, and withdrew his blessings. The son fled and never returned to the old city.

With time and despite some difficulties, Nabou had adapted well to the society of Tangier, which, thanks to its cosmopolitanism, had the advantage of being more open than that of Fez. There was even a black teacher at the American school. His name was Jim, and Nabou knew him a little. He was a charming man who organized sessions once a week when he would play jazz records after introducing and commenting on them. Nabou went there from time to time with the twins. That is how Hassan was introduced to this music, which he preferred to the Egyptian songs that the national radio broadcast all day. He later learned English from Jim and became his friend. Jim told him he dreamed of going someday to visit the land of his ancestors in Guinea or Mali. He did some research and explained to Hassan that he considered himself an African as well as an American. That day, Hassan suddenly understood what brought them closer. Like Jim, he could call himself both African and Moroccan. It was an amazing revelation for him.

Jim, who wrote about the blues and racial discrimination, felt that black musicians and singers were still victims. He told Hassan about Billie Holiday's tragic life, and they listened to several of her songs. Her hurt, bruised voice, beautiful and moving, spoke of the brutality that Whites exercised with impunity against the black people of America. She had experienced prostitution, drugs, and alcohol at a very young age. And then at age forty-four, she had cirrhosis of the liver. Hassan became aware that racism was not an accident of history, but a calamity that sticks to people's skin, no matter where they are. He spoke about it with Hussein, his twin brother, who, although he listened carefully, could not understand the magnitude of the tragedy that his brother experienced. Hassan, who was very sensitive, sensed it and remembered the Moroccan saying: "Only the skin that has been whipped knows how it feels."

With her gift for languages, Nabou spoke Arabic without an accent, always went out wearing a beautiful djellaba, and, especially during the nights of Ramadan, visited the mosque in the Siaghine district, which is just before the area that descends to the port. The rest of the time, she borrowed books from the French Library and read them with a pencil in her hand, noting sentences that pleased her in a school notebook. In the evening, she read them to her husband and began to speak passionately about the importance of literature. Nabou surprised Amir with her interest and desire to learn. He loved those moments when she shared her discoveries with him. One day she brought home a pocket edition of *The Thousand and One Nights* that she had bought on Rue d'Italie. She began to read a story to Amir, who immediately took up the reading—he knew most of it through storytelling.

The reading became a joyful and exciting game for them. She loved all the spicy details, made faces, then took Amir's hand and laid it on her breasts. Their sessions often ended with sexual acrobatics that made them laugh. Their love was always there; they lived it intensely and didn't rely on routine language to express it. Amir had no doubt about Nabou's feelings toward him. He was so sure that one night he woke her up, kissed her hand, and made a statement: "Nabou, you are my life. I hope I deserve your love!" Feeling flustered, Nabou didn't say anything, kissed both his hands, and fell asleep in his arms.

The next day Amir went to the station to meet Moulay Ahmad, who was going to take the boat a few days later to go to Algeciras and to the Lanjaron spa station in Spain, where he was planning to meet friends who were suffering from rheumatism. He invited Amir home, and Amir thought it appropriate to tell him how much he was in love with Nabou. The old sage looked at him severely and said: "She makes you happy in bed, that's all. Do not confuse this with love. Beware of women; they can destroy tomorrow what they love today! Love, what is it? Did your parents love each other like characters in romance books? You're losing your head and mixing the sexual pleasure that this woman gives you with the noble and rare feeling that is called love, which does not need to be trumpeted on the rooftops and in the streets of the medina! Be cautious, my friend, and control yourself!" Then, observing the couple together, he regretted his speech. There was, indeed, love between them, and it moved him so much that after his evening prayer, he clasped his hands and asked God to protect them and save them from the evil that surrounded them.

Hassan and Hussein were attending the French Regnault School in Tangier when some officers and students, who left early in the morning from the Ahermoumou barracks, tried to kill the king. They committed a massacre at the king's birthday party in Skhirat. This first failed coup d'état was repeated a year later in 1972. These crises that started in the mid-sixties pushed Morocco into a period of turbulence that didn't seem to have any end. Amir advised his children to be careful and not get involved with politics. A hunt for political opponents was launched. There were arrests and, sometimes, disappearances. Nabou was afraid because she felt that deep down Hassan was a rebel.

At high school, Hassan didn't work as hard as his brother. He was the only Black in this school where the majority of students were white and French. There was Salem, the son of a Martiniquais and a Moroccan, but he had fair skin. The twins stuck together and didn't mix with other students; they always arrived at school and left together. Their father went out less and less and stayed with Nabou, who liked to pamper him. Amir's back pain forced him to stay in his room. He had trouble getting up and walking. His health was slowly declining, and Nabou hid herself to cry. When the East Wind* arrived in Tangier, everyone in the house became nervous and grumpy. The twins fled to the cinema.

Within a few months, Amir's health deteriorated completely. The doctors, who now had to see him at home, could not determine what was killing him. He was losing weight and his taste for life. Nabou prayed morning and evening, asking God to let Amir live a little longer. Karim could sense that misfortune was approaching their home. He had some terrible presentiments. So every time he saw Amir, he hugged his father's weakened body tightly against his own and told him how much he loved him. Uncle Brahim was taking care of his brother's business. He had found a great solution that assured the family of money. The shop wouldn't carry any more electronic devices bought from the Indians, but would now offer cosmetics imported from Europe and America. It was a unique shop in Tangier, and women queued for its perfumes and creams; fashion magazines never ceased to boast about their benefits. Hussein and Hassan were assisted by their little cousin, Brahim's youngest child.

On the eve of Amir's death, Karim broke down in sobs that could not be stopped. Before everyone else, he knew that the time had arrived. He dared not enter the room where his father was dying in Nabou's arms.

Hassan and Hussein, seeing the state of their brother, understood. Uncle Brahim was called. It was he who was in charge of holding the index finger of Amir's right hand to recite the Shahada, the final words of every Muslim: "I testify that there is no god but God and that Muhammad is his Prophet."

It had not been possible to wait for the arrival of Amir's two sons who were studying in Cairo. As for his daughter, she arrived at night with her unpleasant husband, who didn't bother concealing his racism and arrogance. It was necessary, according to tradition, to bury the body on the day of death. Uncle Brahim took care of everything. Nabou looked dignified in her mourning clothes; she was beginning to have some gray hair, not due to age but more as a result of the ordeals, the humiliations, the wanton insults in the streets or in the market. It had been a long time now since she reacted to them. She held back her anger and concentrated on what was beautiful and good in her life. She knew how to put distance between herself and those attacking her. She held no grudges, prayed in silence before falling asleep, thought of the baobab tree that she secretly called for help. Thanks to the attachment to her traditions, her intelligence, and her patience, she resisted and, as her husband had advised her, preferred to focus on the qualities of people rather than see their flaws and vices. Now that Amir was gone, what would become of her? She gazed tenderly at her children and took Karim in her arms; he had always been her support and accomplice.

Nabou was dressed in white to accompany her husband to the cemetery, but Brahim had to explain to her that in Morocco, women were not allowed to follow the funeral cortege. That's how it was. She could go to Amir's grave whenever she wanted later on. She cried and stayed back with the women who had come to offer condolences.

During the cortege, Hussein noticed two men who were clearly not family members. Hassan leaned over and whispered in his ear: "They're cops." It was a practice at that time: the system had to know and control everything. The deplorable state of the graveyard upset the twins: plastic bags, empty bottles, paper, shit, dog droppings, and cats, even mares. At the entrance, young black boys offered to water the graves. In fact, they were beggars. Someone gave them one or two coins. Immediately, other, white beggars and Koranic readers drove them away with stones. At that moment, Hassan remembered his uncle Hafid, who had gone to live in Sweden because he thought Morocco was far too violent. How right he was, Hassan told himself.

The funeral was too quick, and it shocked the twins. One would have thought it was necessary to finish it as swiftly as possible, to cover the body in its white shroud, to put the slabs on, to join them with cement, to cover the grave with dirt, and to raise joined hands and say the burial prayers.

When everything was finished, one man handed out round bread and dried figs to all. On his way out, Brahim paid the gravediggers and handed out coins. And then they went back home.

The fateful moment arrived. The moment when the absent is present in everybody's minds. During the burial, Nabou had taken care to cover all the mirrors in the house with white sheets, and the television, too. She had prepared a very simple meal for the guests: bread, butter, and honey. Some spoke about Amir, others talked about the price of the land that had increased, and some ventured in a low voice to comment on the future of the beautiful Black. There seemed to be candidates ready to marry her within the week! How things had changed since the death of Lalla Fatma. It was one of those very strange moments. Sadness was in order, but not everyone felt the sorrow in the same way. Nabou watched everybody and had no illusions about humanity. The same reaction could have been in her country. The egoism of men knew no limits. Except that here, in Tangier, she found that men lacked elegance and modesty.

And then, everything rushed on. Uncle Brahim took care of the inheritance, which wasn't very much, and it was divided among Amir's six children, plus a small part was given to Nabou. Becoming conscious that she would not get by on her own, she started looking for work. Hussein continued to look after the shop. Karim, who for some time had been discovering a passion for perfume, spent his day at Madani's, the perfume maker located in the Petit Socco. Madani taught him to differentiate between rose and jasmine, amber and musk, sandalwood and other fragrances.

Day after day, he developed a remarkable sense of smell and refined his perception of scents. Appreciated by the boss and searched out by women who came to ask for his advice, he found himself in an enviable position. He, the handicapped child, the boy whom the French doctor wanted to hide in an institution in France, he, lively and sporty, the person who knew absolutely no evil, the intuitive, the sensitive, had finally found his way. He would use his nose. He didn't need to make speeches or write pages, even though he didn't part with the typing machine his uncle from Casablanca had given him. He described perfumes to his customers with his eyes, his expression, with his hands that traced out precise gestures like those of orchestra conductors.

Nabou was happy to see how talented this boy was, that he knew how to seize an opportunity when it appeared. She thought of Amir, who would have been so proud of him. Karim's reputation spread quickly in the city. People spoke about him as though he were a genius. Some even claimed that he knew perfumes better than his boss. Old Madani didn't care;

he was happy to have put this young man on the path of such a special work in which you had to be both a craftsman and an artist. Karim had become both.

Hassan and Hussein, despite their solidarity in any situation, did not share the same worldview. Hassan was obsessed by his origins, by the color of his skin. He wanted to go to Senegal to follow in the footsteps of his mother's family. Each time he saw Nabou, he asked her many questions, which she didn't always answer, at least not in a way that would satisfy him. She didn't want him to stir up the past, which she preferred to see erased. How could she tell him about her broken family, her loneliness, and the men she had known before Amir? How to suddenly talk about these things she had hidden? The traditions of Fez and Islamic morality would condemn them so much. That is why she avoided Hassan's questions, reformulated them, hoping to discourage her overly curious son.

Hussein was more impassive; he was calmer and allowed himself to enjoy life. He was satisfied with the little he was told about his parents' story and was very careful not to upset his brother. At first Hassan helped him at the shop, but Hussein could see very clearly that he was not interested in this work. To sell makeup to women did not motivate Hassan, so he looked for something bigger. One day a young black woman came to the shop. Hassan approached to serve her, but she pushed him away saying, "I want to be served by the owner, not by his servant!" He didn't answer, removed his white smock, and left the store. Later he found out that the woman claimed to be a great cousin of the king and considered herself a princess. She had such a high sense of herself that she went as far as to forget her skin color and despised the poor and the Blacks.

Nabou now managed to earn a little money. She did some sewing, offering a kind of subtle Fassi and Senegalese fusion she designed. Her clients were mainly Europeans who found her original style interesting. Thus, she was introduced to the very closed circle of Tangier's foreign community into which few Moroccans were admitted.

At the home of one of her best clients, Countess Elena Bloomfield, she met Ralph and Juan Carlos, a homosexual couple who lived between Amsterdam and Miami and had just bought an old house in the Casbah. Ralph was a university professor and his partner a dancer in a Colombian troupe that performed a lot in Spain. During a performance at the International Casino of Tangier, Juan Carlos fell in love with the city and decided to buy property. They needed someone they could trust to look after their house while they were away. They came mostly in the summer and sometimes in the spring. Nabou was exactly the person they were looking for. "You can continue to do your sewing," they said. "The important thing is to open the windows often because of the humidity, to keep the whole house clean, and to prepare it a few days before our arrival. If you wish, we can also allow you to stay there, you and your children; there is plenty of room. When we stay there, you'll take care of everything, do grocery shopping and cook for us, that is, if you accept our offer."

Nabou spoke to her children, who welcomed the news. Karim told her that he would never leave her. Hussein answered her by saying: "Why not!" As for Hassan, he assured her of his support and simply asked for her blessing, to which he attached great importance: it offered him a share of the magic and mystery that only he understood.

Ralph and Juan Carlos's house overlooked the sea, but it needed to be completely renovated. In the winter, as she had been asked, Nabou lit the chimneys to fight against the humidity. She cleaned the house regularly and prepared the rooms as if the owners could arrive any moment. Sometimes she would stop in front of an unmade bed. She would think of the happy hours she had lived with Amir and cried silently. She never spoke about her memories in front of others.

One day, while cleaning the house, Nabou accidentally broke a beautiful Famille Rose Canton porcelain vase. She was very worried and didn't know how to repair the damage caused by her clumsiness. It was impossible to glue the vase back together. Not knowing what to do, she went to an antique shop in search of a similar vase. This is how she met Sidi Boubker, who had a shop on Rue de la Liberté. When she entered, he was in the back of his shop, immersed in reading the Koran. He had heard about Nabou because Ralph and Juan Carlos were his customers. She told him about her accident. Sidi Boubker, a generous and good man, reassured her:

"I know very well which vase it is. It was a pair, but Ralph was only interested in one. I have the other, perfectly identical to the one that broke. Take it, and I'll take care of it with Ralph. Above all, don't try to pay me. I'll know how to settle this with your employer; he's my friend. Anyway, it's too expensive. Come on, I'll ask Mohamed to wrap it up. Keep it in a safe place, so that it doesn't break before they return. The day before their arrival, place it in the same spot as the other. It will be our secret."

Nabou didn't know how to thank Sidi Boubker. Other than Amir, she had never met such a generous man. The following day, she returned with a beautiful scarf she had embroidered and offered it to him: "This is for your wife. I hope she'll like it." Leaving the shop, she said to herself: Fortunately, there are men of this quality; these are true Muslims.

But on her way back, she had not taken three steps out of the shop when a short, skinny, gray man started to harass her:

"I'll denounce you! I'll denounce you! You killed Lalla Fatma, you poisoned her."

Nabou hurried on. He started to follow her and continued to accuse her by shouting out some troubling details. At one moment, catching sight of a police officer, Nabou uttered a scream and that immediately drove the intrusive man away. But she could sense that he would come back soon to blackmail her.

The following week, the short gray man knocked on the door of the villa. It was Hassan who opened it. He immediately knew who the man was, as his mother had described him. He rushed toward him, lifted him from the ground, and said firmly:

"If you ever come near my mother, I swear I'll squish you like a fly, like a cockroach, you sleazebag. Another thing, this neighborhood, as long as I'm alive, is forbidden to you. These are not empty words, it's an order."

Then Hassan dropped him on the ground. The short gray man got his feet caught in a garbage can, fell, got up, and fled. They never saw him again.

In the evening, Nabou talked about the incident to Karim. He stood in front of his writing machine and wrote a letter to the short man: "Life is beautiful, and you, not beautiful!"

One day, Hussein came home and wanted to say something to his mother. He hesitated for a moment and then announced the news:

"I am getting married!"

Nabou continued to scrub the floor with an American product that made it shine quickly and well. Without looking at his face, she said:

"That's good, my son. But your brother? Have you thought about him?"

"Don't you want to know to whom I'm getting married?"

"Yes, of course. But I'm worried about your brother."

For her, the twins had to get married on the same day to respect the tradition and also because of her modest means. If Hussein got married before Hassan, her black son would once again experience discrimination. He would suffer, especially since Hussein was too busy with his business lately to give his brother moral support.

Hussein wasn't listening to his mother; he wanted to tell her that he had finally found the woman of his life. She came from a big family in Tangier, and he was eager to legalize this relationship.

When Nabou shared the news with Hassan, he understood his mother's wish and promised that he would do everything to find a woman as soon as possible. He didn't want to discuss with her the numerous racist incidents he had experienced. Such incidents were generally accepted by all and didn't seem to bother anyone. But Hassan never got used to them and often repeated to his brother:

"The heart must either break or turn to lead; me, I break my heart a little every day!"

Later on, Hussein informed him about his plans to get married. Hassan hugged him tightly and wished him happiness. He, too, had a secret, a much more serious one: he had a son with a foreign woman, Mina, a biracial woman who worked at the Spanish consulate. It was not a love story; they met at a party where everyone danced and drank a lot. He had pulled her against him; she had pressed her warm lips on his. Hassan, who knew the house well, had taken her to the master bedroom, where they had made love several times without even talking to each other. It was only a physical attraction. Two bodies that needed to meet and merge. The next day they parted feeling that they had made a bad mistake.

One day, Mina arrived, radiant, at the shop and told Hassan that she was pregnant and that she had no intention of having an abortion. She had not asked him for anything; she reassured him that she was happy to carry this child. Disturbed and worried, Hassan said nothing to anyone and waited impatiently for the child's birth. It was a boy with skin as black as his father's.

Mina had to give him up under the pressure of her parents as well as the consular authorities that threatened to lay her off. By mutual agreement, she and Hassan entrusted the baby to the Spanish sisters who had an association for unmarried mothers in the Marchane neighborhood. By slipping a few banknotes in the *adouls'* pockets, Hassan acknowledged him and named him Salim. He thus had a birth certificate that said, "Mother died at childbirth." Hassan told the sisters that one day he would come and take him back. That day had arrived.

When Hassan told his mother about his son, she burst into tears and reproached him for not having told her right away:

"How old is he?"

"A year."

"I would have been so happy! Do you realize, I was a grandmother and I didn't know it! Bring the little one to me; it's a marvel, a gift from God. But why don't you marry his mother?"

He explained that it was complicated, that her family was Catholic and very conservative, and that the consulate would disapprove. He confessed that they were not in love and that, in any case, if Mina wanted to see her son, there would be no problem. Recently, however, he learned that she had left with her parents without leaving an address, probably for Cuba, where she was from.

Hassan, therefore, began looking for a wife. He remembered that one of his cousins, a projectionist in a cinema in the Fez New Town, had married by publishing an advertisement in an Egyptian cinema magazine called *Kawakeb*. A young woman who limped, but it was not visible in the photo, responded to his announcement. They met after the projection of a black-and-white film in which Farid El Atrache played a seducer without success and lamented by singing syrupy and boring litanies. They commented on the film and laughed. The next day they met at the place of an *adoul*, who married them.

Hassan wanted to try his luck, but the magazine in question no longer existed. There was a program on Radio Tangier called "Friendship Links." He followed it and that's how he got married to Zineb, a woman who was divorced because she couldn't have children. She was quite pretty and her skin was almost black. She was a teacher at the French school Berchet. When Hassan informed her that he already had a son, she proposed to raise him as if he were her own. But Nabou really wanted to take care of him herself.

Salim was a gifted child. He understood everything very quickly, but he was lazy and rather capricious. Nabou spoiled him, and his father couldn't do anything about it. He wasn't very good in his studies and barely passed to the upper class. One day, his father scolded him, and Salim asked: "What's the use of learning things I already know?"

Salim, after all, was a fighter. He fought back at the slightest racist remark. He was a rebel, which his father secretly admired.

Chapter 6

Tangier, 2010. There was something Hassan enjoyed: borrowing the German car from his brother and taking his son, Salim, for a ride on the city's new ring road. The road started at the port and went along the sea to the Jewish River, a popular neighborhood. He would sometimes stop and observe the view from behind the Casbah. On the cliff he could see some shacks with tin roofs and also the houses overlooking the ocean where the Atlantic begins. There was the famous house of Yves and Charles, the York Castle, now in ruins; the Forbes Palace; the terraces of the Café Hafa; and the small palaces belonging to some celebrities. Hassan liked to find Ralph and Juan Carlos's house, which was hard to see. Often, he briefly waved, as if his mother were at the window and could see him.

Paul Bowles was dead now, as were most people of his generation who used to meet up in Tangier to smoke and get laid with "cheap boys," as Beat poet Allen Ginsberg called them. The city had changed. In the sumptuous houses recently renovated by decorators and artists from London and elsewhere, there was no longer the spirit of the old Tangier with its myths and legends. And the unexpected arrival of sub-Saharan young people who had missed their crossing to Europe had changed the city's face and body . . .

The East Wind blew harder and harder; the city had lost something. Some would say it was charm; others would speak of a hurt soul, a memory filled with holes. The industrial zone was now vast, and it polluted Tangier with impunity.

Nabou was still busy taking care of Ralph and Juan Carlos's house. Her advanced age and rheumatism made her tired. Hassan and Karim helped her on her deep-cleaning days. Salim made her somewhat anxious. Sometimes he would cry and ask for his mother. Nabou consoled him by saying how much she loved him. Zineb, his father's wife, was often insensitive toward him. Her relationship with Hassan was fragile and satisfied her less and less. One day, overwhelmed by this situation, she took her things and went back to live with her parents.

As for Hussein, he was home less and less often. His shop was never empty. He had plans to open another on Boulevard Pasteur and hoped to get his twin brother interested. But Hassan was overwhelmed by so many questions that he couldn't do anything else. Little by little, he felt as though he was becoming one of those Blacks who roamed around in the cemeteries. Worn down by his failures, he had become, over the years, a very somber man, very withdrawn.

Hassan spent most of his days walking alone around the city without any real purpose. When he walked, he often came across African beggars. They were always more numerous in Tangier. He had heard rumors that there were no more cats in town because they ate them. The rumors varied from one café to another, from one hammam to another.

One day during his walk, he paused for a long time and, leaning against a pillar, stared at a man who must have been his age; Hassan looked at him insistently and with sympathy; then, concentrating, he imagined himself in the man's skin. He saw himself in the streets looking for work or some coins to buy food. Hassan had this secret ability to project himself into the lives of others and into the most complex situations. He had briefly dreamed of becoming a comedian, but there was no place in Tangier to learn, much less practice, this profession. Suddenly, he felt a cold fever rise within him. Sweat beaded on his forehead. His sight was blurry. His tongue was frozen. His whole body was undergoing a strange transformation. His black skin shone, and he felt convinced he was wearing a white mask. A heavy silence prevailed all around, as though he had been removed from the life that surrounded him and as though his skin was changing. Surrounded by this silence, as in a soundless show, he was beside himself.

He tried to react but felt that his movements were slow and his voice distant. The Africans around him smiled despite their distress. They were laughing, making noise, but he could hear nothing. He was now part of this group while a stranger to himself. He began to move forward and headed for the taxi stand down the Rue de Fès. He felt as if he was being pulled by something. Hassan said to himself: It's the call of destiny, I can feel it, I'm sure of it.

After suddenly returning to himself, he went to a street and hailed a shared taxi, a big yellow Mercedes dating back several decades, and said to the driver, "Take me to Saddam." After a while he asked the driver, "By the way, why does the neighborhood bear this name?" A bearded man in a white djellaba replied: "Saddam, like Saddam Hussein. He is a martyr. He was humiliated and then murdered by the Americans. He was a great patriot who fought against Iran for his Arab brothers, and then his Arab brothers sold him, abandoned him. That's why our neighborhood deserves the name of Saddam . . . And we are proud to have given it his name . . . At home, in Africa, you have no Saddam, you have Bokassa?" A great laughter ensued.

Hassan could have reminded him about the crimes that Saddam committed against his people, but talking to a bearded man seemed useless, so he said to himself: It starts with *salamalecs** and then it degenerates . . . I don't want to justify myself . . . The bearded guy has his own convictions, and I have mine. It's useless to confront them, and anyway, he has already labeled me. I am African. With these people, it's best not to argue, either we agree with them or we shut up . . . Here's proof that we are not democrats. The neighbor who refuses to lower the sound of his television is of the same kind: egotistical, intolerant, and arrogant. He also puts Islam in all the sauces. And then there is another who allows himself not to pay the charges for his apartment because he believes that everything is due him. Or there is this lawyer, known for losing all his cases, who wants to follow the law and prevent unmarried couples from living in his building. He, too, is part of this league of virtue against vice. It was impossible to have discussions; there was no freedom to express an opposite point of view. Hassan knew what to expect. Islam was a convenient scapegoat. He would have liked to explain to them that they confused everything and excused their stupidity in the name of Islam, which had nothing to do with their egotistical and fanatical behaviors. He said to himself: In this taxi there is Morocco with its believers and its opportunists, with its prejudices and outrages, and then there is me, who is not a good Muslim and who cannot say it, and who is perceived like a stranger from the Sahel*. There is my desire to confront these people, and, at the same time, there is the reality that I would not win any victory. On the contrary, they would lynch me if they could. It is better to keep quiet, keep a low profile, and forget about it.

He was in his thoughts when the driver shouted to him:

"Hey you, Kahlouch*, we've arrived, get out."

"Kahlouch," that is to say, Negro, slave, in Arabic . . . Hassan had heard this insult so often that he no longer reacted to it. He could have responded, "You Khoroto," the name given to white Moroccans who are losers, but it was useless. Khoroto! The important thing that day was to go see for himself in what conditions sub-Saharans lived in Morocco.

After walking around a bit in the Saddam district, Hassan found a café across from one of the main squats and settled down. Not far from him, someone was saying that a fight had broken out the day before between the quiet Africans and the newcomers. It was a question of toilets. The new chief had decided that no one had the right to use his toilet. "Otherwise?" someone asked loudly. "Otherwise, I'll cut off your dick!" He didn't seem to be joking.

Hassan was in a part of the city where the police came only occasionally. It had been like this for a few years now. The people had organized themselves. There were chiefs, and a certain order reigned there as long as no one tried to upset the so-called "Boss."

The Boss was short and fat, with green eyes and wrinkles all over his face. Impossible to give him an age. He was the most important man in this neighborhood, where he controlled hashish smuggling and selected the girls to send as prostitutes to Malaga and Marbella. The Boss had several nicknames: "Dib" (the wolf), "Manchar" (the saw—it's said he dismembered his victims with a saw), "Wazir" (the minister, because he rode in a black limousine with tinted windows), and "Nzak" (mercury, he was hard to catch). He passed through the place unexpectedly and resolved pending issues. Of course, he didn't live there, but even so, he wanted to have his own toilet; no one knew where he lived. He was extremely well protected, and when one of his guards stepped out of line, he made him disappear. It was said that if he said to you, "Tonight we're going fishing together," it meant your last hour had arrived.

One day, when the Boss was in charge of another squat owned by one of his associates who had died of a heart attack, he caught one of his men giving information to a plainclothes police officer. He let the man go on and changed all his own plans. He summoned his young cousin, who was barely twenty years old, put a revolver in his hand, and ordered him to shoot "the traitor." The kid refused. He snatched the weapon from his hand and put a bullet through both traitors' foreheads. It was the first day of Ramadan, on the cliff of Rmilat, which faces the meeting point of the Atlantic and the Mediterranean.

The Boss was sometimes "generous" toward the unfortunate Africans who had nothing and begged in Tangier's streets. He would charter a boat, which he filled with about fifty men and women, and, in exchange for a small fee, gave orders that they be taken to Spain. Once they were at sea, he would ask one of his men to inform the Guardia Civil of Almería . . . Passengers were greeted on arrival by an army of police and Spanish gendarmes to whom they surrendered without resistance. They were then sent back to their country after being detained a few days in a detention center.

From time to time in these neighborhoods, deprived Moroccan squatters declared war on the Africans. Tangier then showed its ugliest and most disturbing face. This Tangier was unknown; it was not part of the landscape. Poor and miserable, chaotic and delinquent, marginal and corrupt—no one would have thought of going to this part of the city. Hassan knew about it, but he had so far been too scared to acknowledge the situation. Perhaps because of his skin color, he stayed away from that other body of Tangier, that other face full of holes and pus. Yet he felt close to it, a Black among Blacks;

he knew that nothing separated him from these undocumented, illegal immigrants, victims of misery, in precarious exile and constantly under threat.

He had talked about it with his brother, Hussein. For him, this place was a hell devoid of rules, of all rules. It was the realm of the strongest. The Mafia was complicit with elements of the police and the gendarmerie. Hussein, he preferred to sell his makeup products to the women who walked into his shop, and some of them waited for it to close, when they would rush inside and take off their djellabas. One day, he told his nephew about a husband who barged in shouting like crazy. Hussein asked him to lower his voice. The man was furious. He reproached him for selling a fragrance to his wife that attracted men, and he was afraid of being cuckolded. Everyone started laughing. An aged woman had wanted to buy this miracle perfume. The husband went off cursing. Hussein, in his youth, had lived a fallen life, the opposite of his twin brother. A bon vivant, he did not feel responsible for anything.

Recently the king decided to strike a big blow in the north of Tangier to spread panic among kif traffickers. A major operation followed. But the police were disappointed; they found only minor traffickers there. The real chiefs had taken their precautions and disappeared overnight.

Hassan came out of the café and resumed his walk. The Saddam neighborhood didn't have any charm. It was designed haphazardly and built in a hurry. Not a single tree in the main square. All cut down. You have to be rich to enjoy a green space. Most of the buildings were unfinished. Not even whitewash on the facades: one could see the naked red bricks, some of which were cracked. And there were cafés everywhere, built under sheds and open to the streets, with Formica tables and plastic chairs as the only furniture. Fruit and vegetable vendors spread their produce on the ground. Fishermen shouted, "Fresh sardine, *sardine fresca*, sardine caught today, ten dirhams." A guy a little farther away was selling shaving cream, plastic flowers, and clocks with a picture of the Kaaba* on their faces. An African was selling trinkets from his country next to a boy offering retail cigarettes, and another was selling pirated DVDs. A butcher was grilling sheep heads, and a parking attendant was calling the shots.

Hassan widened his eyes and wondered if he was still in Tangier. A mosque in the middle of the main street, no school or pharmacy. Men dressed in afghans, in long black tunics, gray *taguia* on their heads, were walking around, some of them followed by women dressed all in black. He wasn't too surprised. He had heard about these people who practiced an Islam made up by ignorant people.

He went around the neighborhood and saw other Africans who sold boxes of Kleenex, fake Louis Vuitton bags, or Chinese products. Some were sitting together on the ground as if waiting for a bus, a train, or, better still, a prophet who would rescue them from there, take them away, far from this little, daily hell. But Hassan knew that no saint or prophet would think of stopping there and that no one would be saved.

Hassan had strong intuitions that he received like messages. This mixture of colors and spices, these not-so-good smells, this agitation penetrated from time to time by the call to prayer made him feel beside himself for the second time that day. He felt once again that he no longer belonged. A charlatan, a sort of hypnotist without talent, stood before him and shouted that the end of the world was imminent, that it was necessary to give up vices and return to the essential virtues, which were taught by the Prophet of all times, the only one who would intercede in favor of the nonbelievers, those who have their hearts and the bodies ravaged by Evil . . . The charlatan suddenly stopped screaming and pointed a threatening finger at a group of Africans terrorized by his speech: "They are as black as sin, as black as the night of crime, as black as the great door to hell . . ." The Africans looked at each other and preferred to ignore him.

At Ralph and Juan Carlos's place, Hassan sometimes met a sophisticated crowd of posh people, good-natured, well-off, and proud of their festive extravagance. He had seen time and again how Tangier was a complex city, flirting with perversities and contradictions that only the East Wind could manage to calm. Where was his place? Who was he? He was so silent, unable to say what haunted him; he had always felt left to himself, without any bearings. He often thought about his father, who left too early and whose grave he never visited. He also thought of his mother, whom he loved so much. Suddenly, Nabou's face, so black, so brilliant, imposed itself on him, like an image in a waking dream. It looked like she was sitting on a wall munching on a stick of licorice, looking absent, as if she was not expecting anything or anyone. And the more he watched the men squatting under the sun, the clearer and bigger the image of the beautiful African lady became. She was smiling; maybe she was waving at him to join her.

The charlatan came back to Hassan and told him confidently: "Beware of these Blacks, they are the offspring of Satan. You are not a real Black, you wear a white mask, and it is seen from afar. Everyone is talking about Bilal, the black slave who was freed by our beloved Prophet. But these Blacks are not believers like you, some carry a cross, others pray in front of trees; they must go home, and they should not be here. There is enough misery with us here . . ."

Hassan didn't answer him, running his hand over his face as if he wanted to make sure he wasn't wearing a mask. He then moved away and was again struck by a strange feeling: And what if one of these men were my second cousin, a brother, and a relative, someone whose genes I carry and look like? And if it were I sitting, watching the horizon, and waiting for a miracle? And what if the chosen tribe's hope and honor lay with me to attempt the journey to paradise? Yes, it's me; it's really me. My skin is black, quite black, it doesn't fear the sun, it shines at her touch . . . I am African. I walked days and nights in the sands, crossed mountains, lakes, and forests. I am a clandestine, the chief clandestine. I know where I come from, but I don't know where to go . . .

Hassan avoided getting in a shared taxi. He had heard enough hideous comments on his way there and didn't want to hear new ones. He walked along the road, didn't look back, and thought about his son, Salim. He wondered whether his son was strong enough to endure this wanton hatred, whether he was sufficiently armed to defend himself against imbeciles, and he blamed himself for not having prepared him to live in a country where being black was hard luck. That evening, he talked to Salim about it and told him about the Saddam neighborhood and what he saw there. Salim had just turned twenty, was still trying to find himself, wanted to study medicine but was not up to the competition. He was quite attracted by journalism. With his savings, he had bought a Canon camera, and, from time to time, did photo shoots that he showed to a local newspaper director, who encouraged him to continue in this way. When he felt he had some strong images, he posted them on the social networks.

One morning, Salim thought back about the conversation he had with his father, took his camera, and decided to go see for himself what was going on in those suburbs that were said to be the worst. On Fez Street, he jumped into a shared taxi and said, "To Saddam." He heard the driver say in Arabic that Salim was going to join his lost brothers, those who would do better to go back to their jungle because Morocco has enough problems with Moroccans, and it cannot accommodate all the desperate of the world . . . Salim didn't react. But when he arrived at the entrance of the neighborhood, he found himself having the same thought as the driver: Why were these men and women living in this misery? He started walking, his right hand clutching his camera, watching the world he had imagined, but found it even more distressing than he thought. The lack of hygiene, the dirt on the unpaved streets, the cooking smells, the heat, and the white sky gave him the impression of being far from his country.

He was lost in his thoughts when he heard a scream followed by the sound of something falling. Immediately, a panic-stricken crowd rushed toward it. There was a pool of blood on the ground. In the middle lay a man, a black man, his head and chest smashed. Salim pushed the crowd aside and approached the still-breathing body. He screamed, "Call an ambulance! Call the police!"

The police weren't far away. They had been looking for a Guinean suspected of having been involved in the burglary of an American's villa. They ended up finding him here, in an unfinished building, which was one of the most important squats in the neighborhood. The police had been searching and systematically returning to this place.

Among the redbrick structures, large holes opened in the void; they were awkwardly arranged as a space of survival, and he could not escape the police. When the suspect finally saw them coming, threatening him with clubs, he began to run, tripped on a bag of cement that lay ripped open, lost his balance, and fell from the fourth floor.

This man moved to the Saddam district only recently. He had lived in a forest for a long time; it had a strange name, "Diplomatique." The forest was located about twenty kilometers from the center of Tangier, not far from the Atlantic. There, along with others, he managed to get by, went fishing, and slept in a hut. The rest of the time, he went to the roadside and begged. Some motorists, mostly Moroccan immigrants who were returning to Europe, sometimes stopped and gave him food or some coins. But one day, some local families, who used to picnic in the forest, called on the police to get rid of these illegal immigrants, accusing them of being carriers of diseases that threatened to become epidemic. When the police arrived, the young Guinean and his gang immediately fled and took refuge in a Spanish Catholic church located near the Hasnouna neighborhood. The priest, a Black from Brazil, welcomed them but warned: "This is temporary, and I cannot keep you for a long time, but rest, we will give you something to eat, you can wash up in the room at the entrance. God is with you, my brothers." One of the men got up to thank him and said: "We would like you to tell our Moroccan brothers that not all Moroccans are racists, but as a saying from our homeland goes: 'All you need is one carious tooth to spoil all the others.'" When ordered to leave the church, the small gang landed a few days later in the big squat of the Saddam neighborhood. Fights had immediately broken out between the new and the old Africans, to which the Moroccans there didn't react.

It was in this heated atmosphere, which lasted for several days, that the police intervened, allegedly in search of a Guinean suspected of burglary.

His body now lay almost lifeless, covered with mud and blood. Salim was still there, next to the man, leaning over him in shock. Not the others, who must have been used to these kinds of incidents. He didn't even think of taking pictures.

Police officers who had come to reinforce order in the situation dispersed the onlookers, but arrested a few Blacks who were still around because they didn't have the reflex to flee. When the ambulance finally arrived, it was already too late.

This is how Salim found himself with five Africans in the Tangier police van; the police roughly pushed them onto the ground, tied their hands, took their pictures at the nearest police station, and then made them board a bus bound for Casablanca, where a plane already half-filled with other migrants was waiting to transport them to Senegal.

Salim's camera was confiscated. He protested at first, said it was his work tool, claimed he was Moroccan, his father from Fez and his mother a Senegalese, but no one paid any attention to him. They hit him on the back of the neck and Salim thought he heard an officer say, "All Moroccans are Africans, but not all Africans are Moroccans." As for the other arrested Africans, they regarded Salim as a traitor, someone who denied his ethnicity and wanted to pretend to be a White, an Arab, a Moroccan from the city of spirituality and the crucible of the Arab-Andalusian civilization. All of a sudden Salim felt ashamed. His Africanity was evident, visible, obvious, and he could neither deny nor condemn it. His fate was sealed.

Salim realized that his skin color had already condemned him and that no word could do anything about it. It was thus better to stop protesting. For the first time he lived in his body and his skin. His hands were tied, the bus was driving at full speed, but he had changed. In any case, he didn't have any identification document proving he was who he claimed to be. He remained silent, tried to close his eyes and let his mind go blank. His head was empty. No picture, no sound, nothing, not even a memory. As though a wall had collapsed. The other Africans were sleeping. They were probably tired, broken by this kind of treatment, resigned, their minds elsewhere. Salim couldn't close his eyes. He watched the trees go by, the sky disappearing as his breathing became slower and slower.

They arrived in Casa at night. The plane was waiting for them. The police had reserved the rows at the back. They went in through the back door, still handcuffed, accompanied by an officer who was scolding them because he had no desire to go on this forced trip, especially at night. They were given a roll and a bottle of water. Most went back to a deep sleep. Salim, he remained awake.

Everything was mixed up in his head. He had learned quite a lot about the presence of Blacks in Morocco; he had discovered that Ahmad al-Mansour Al-dhahabi, who had reigned from 1578 to 1603 and was the famous hero of the Battle of the Three Kings, had not only defeated the Portuguese army, but also killed their king, Sebastian, who had a black mother, a Peul named Lalla 'Awda. Someone had told Salim that Hassan II's grandmother was black. There was no written record of this story, which was an unverifiable rumor. There was also the one whom the French press called the "black pearl," the great football player Larbi Ben Barek.

And then there was this black minister, a companion and faithful friend of King Hassan II, who had finished his career as the Moroccan ambassador to the United Nations . . . Famous Blacks and anonymous Blacks had always lived in this country, prisoners of a kind of denial or amnesia. So much racism, so much stupidity found justification in a supposed superiority of the Arabs over the Africans, in old reflexes inherited from colonial behaviors. This racism, present since the dawn of time, in all Moroccan social strata, had exploded at the turn of the 2000s with the regular arrival of more and more migrants trying to cross the Strait of Gibraltar. Salim knew all this but had never imagined that one day he would find himself in this situation, which he faced with a calm that surprised him.

Nonetheless, Salim dreaded the arrival in Dakar. He heard one of the police officers say hatefully: "Back to the sender! No place for you here!" Then he hummed an old song: "Black is black! Black is black!" . . . He was singing it out of tune, yet it made no one laugh.

At the airport, the border police greeted them with insults. Salim didn't understand the language they spoke. As he was the best dressed, an officer took him for a band leader and spoke to him in French:

"So, didn't you manage to take your friends to paradise?"

"The doors to paradise are closed . . ."

"You want to be funny? Last name, first name, place of birth."

Salim tried to tell him the truth, but he was not believed. He swore that his arrest was a mistake. He reclaimed his camera that a Tangier cop had confiscated. He received a punch along with insults:

"You dirty Negro! You, Moroccan? You, Muslim? You, from a grand family? Aren't you ashamed to lie and pretend to be what you're not, what you'll never be! Have you ever seen an illegal immigrant with a camera? Me, I've never seen one!"

It was only the following day that their handcuffs were removed and they were allowed to go.

And so Salim, hungry, penniless, and humiliated, discovered his grand-mother's birthplace. He wanted to wash up and sleep. So he entered a small mosque and used the bathroom to wash himself and make his ablutions. He prayed a little without words—he had forgotten the verses—and then he leaned against a pillar and fell deeply asleep. No one disturbed him. He was so hungry that for the first time in his life he went out to beg in the streets. The city looked modern and reminded him of Casablanca: well-designed large avenues, very tall buildings. This was his first surprise. He spoke to people in French, but they were too rushed and didn't pay attention to him. He found himself at Independence Square, not far from the train station and the port. Street vendors hawked items imported from China: sunglasses, dolls, toys, scarves, fans . . . One of them started harassing him: "Here, my brother, a luxury watch, cheap, very cheap, a perfume for your wife, a belt for your mistress . . ." In other circumstances, Salim would have laughed at him, but he didn't want to. As the vendor kept insisting, Salim turned to him and said, "Leave me in peace, you're a pain in the ass!" The man didn't appreciate it at all and replied, "I'm clingy, not a pain in the ass! Don't insult me in this way!" Salim burst out laughing and asked to be taken to his boss to offer his services. The guy didn't appreciate it, moved to another side-walk, and disappeared.

Tangier, his native hometown, suddenly seemed to him like a planet very far away. His memories became blurry. From time to time the faces of his grandmother, his father, and Karim furtively appeared to him. He would have so liked to hold them, caress them, and find those peaceful moments that sometimes reigned in the big house. He thought he heard Hassan's voice telling him to go to a place of prayer. He entered a church, where a priest gave him some food and didn't ask him any questions. It was better that way. For a while he thought about presenting himself at the Moroc-can consulate, but he had no documents to prove his nationality. In a way, he liked this situation that put him to the test. To be African, poor, and defenseless, without family and without hope, was it not the destiny of millions of people on this continent that is rich and poor at the same time? So he decided not to change his condition and to follow his destiny to the end. Insults and banal racism, he knew them. He wanted to live from within what those like him experienced daily.

The priest, who realized that Salim spoke perfect Arabic, put him in touch with Abdallah, an imam who hadn't mastered the language of the Koran. For a little money, Salim helped him learn to pronounce the words in certain prayers better. He was happy to render service to this man, whose wisdom and willpower he appreciated, but he never ceased thinking about going back to the same conditions as his fellow men, some of whom came to meet at the mosque. He wanted to make the trip, the long and perilous journey, cross the Sahara, arrive in the south of Morocco, and go back to Tangier from where illegal immigrants went to Spain. Day after day, it became his obsession, his madness.

Back in Tangier, Salim's family was very worried. The police said they didn't know anything about this matter. Hassan was promised they would post his photo at police stations and border posts. Karim was so miserable that he lost his sense of smell for a few days. Nabou could guess that her grandson was in Africa; she remembered a discussion with him when he planned to go on this trip one day. But that didn't lessen her worries. She had heard the news of the death of the unfortunate Guinean in the neighborhood of Saddam without making any connection with Salim's disappearance.

Karim woke up Nabou one night saying:

"I saw, I have . . . I have . . . saw Salim. Mu-muezzin, mosque in your country!"

He was filled with emotion by his vision and felt reassured of his nephew's safety.

Nabou thanked him and imagined Salim making the call to prayer in a mosque in Dakar. After all, she asked herself, why not?

Karim and Nabou were not totally wrong. At the same moment in Dakar, Salim was teaching Abdallah the Moroccan way of calling the faithful to prayer.

Thanks to his job with the imam, Salim stayed clean, ate his fill, and found pleasure in discovering this city. He felt like looking for traces of his grandmother, to find someone who knew her, but he felt a kind of apprehension and gave up the idea. He was afraid of what he might discover. He also thought of sending a telegram to Tangier to give news, but once he arrived at the post office, he turned around. After a night of reflection, he changed his mind and wrote this text:

"Dear Ma (this is how he called Nabou), dear Father, dear Uncles, I am in Africa, will come home soon, Salim."

It was expensive. He took out "dear Uncles," paid, and the telegram was sent.

The imam was originally from Gorée Island. As he was going to visit his parents, he proposed taking Salim with him and said they would stay in the family house. Salim agreed immediately. On the way there, the imam told him the story of this island, which he had heard from his father's mouth.

Things there had changed a bit since slave-trading times. Even African Americans came there regularly, big fellows who went on pilgrimage to the places of their ancestors, slaves bought to work in the New World. They took pictures, some prayed in silence, as though they were in a church, others remained quiet, distributing one-dollar bills to children and beggars. The face of one of these visitors caught Salim's attention. It felt as if he had seen him somewhere. A movie actor—he had seen him in an action film in which he played the assistant of a white cop . . . Salim made an effort to remember: *Lethal Weapon*, that's it! Danny . . . Danny Glover and Mel Gibson! It was Danny Glover. He was accompanied by another African American who introduced himself to the imam as Manthia Diawara, a professor at New York University. "Today in America," he said, "we are proud of our origins, and by fighting we have obtained some rights . . ."

Even though tourists invaded this island, it had a lot of power. More than just the traces of a shameful past, deeper memory rose proudly to the surface. Salim and the imam left a few days later for Dakar and resumed their work together.

Salim had saved some money by now. He really didn't need to spend much. One evening, while he was in a café and watching television, he saw in the news pictures of migrants drowning in the middle of the Mediterranean. One of them raised both hands and made the V sign of victory. On this day he made a firm decision to go on foot to the north of Morocco with a small group of men his own age whom he had met recently. They had told him that they hoped to succeed in crossing the Strait of Gibraltar to reach Europe.

Salim could have stayed in Dakar, taught French and Arabic, made a quiet little life for himself, and placed a good distance between himself and Morocco, or, to be more exact, some Moroccans. He could have found himself among the African crowd and lived from day to day like most people, but something prevented him from being content with that. He wanted to know what his destiny reserved for him, the one decided by the color of his skin, by chance, and by ordinary, banal, stupid racism. He remembered something his father often used to say to him: "Our destiny is our only baggage. It's the one that carries us and defends us against our own selves."

It was at a café that he met this small group. It seemed like they were plotting; they spoke in low voices, appeared cautious of others, and seemed to be up to some mischief. Salim understood very quickly that they wanted to do what thousands of other Africans had done before them. But almost all were far from succeeding. If some of them were well settled in Europe, many were held in detention centers or prisons, and many more lay at the bottom of the Strait of Gibraltar. Salim told himself he didn't have much to lose. And to try this adventure, despite the risks, didn't scare him. He could have borrowed money from his uncle and bought a plane ticket, gone to the Moroccan consulate and collected his papers to cross the border. Yet he went to sit next to these guys and said, "I'm leaving with you." None of them had any objection. He was one of the many, ready to take the risk.

This project suited Salim. It had been enough for him to come across a few malicious police officers, frustrated and racist, who refused to listen to him, or verify his claims, so that his whole life had been turned upside down. At present, he no longer had any illusions about humanity. He spoke about his upcoming departure to the imam, who tried in vain to dissuade him. Seeing that Salim's determination was firm, the imam gave him some money and prayed for his success.

The members of the small group had already given a part of the amount demanded by the future smuggler to one of his partners, who was settled in Dakar. Salim paid without flinching. He found it very expensive, but said nothing. He thought that the African curse was beginning when he handed over his savings to a dubious person, who had his eyes hidden behind huge, dark glasses and wore a metal bracelet on his wrist engraved with his name, "Sam." The guy was of mixed race; he had tattooed on his forearm a snake gliding between thighs with the inscription "Love." So that was how it all began? Adventure and hope, misfortune and perhaps death? Salim looked hard at the companions with whom he was going to undertake a long, a very long, journey. He drank a big glass of water and said, "Let's go!"

Chapter 7

"It has been so long since I have been walking on the sand that my feet are heavy and don't seem to belong to me anymore. At night, I follow a star that guides my steps and it abandons me in the morning. I walk and I don't turn to look back. That's the rule: if you turn around, you're damned, you'll lose your mind; that's what I was told repeatedly before my departure, and I think it's true. So I walk on without looking back at what I have left behind: my grandmother's country, which didn't look like what I imagined; beautiful trees speaking to me at night; men and women who waved flies and boredom away with their big hands; a white and heavy sky; strange nights when I remained awake; the bitter taste of imported dried figs; the smells of strong spices that insinuated themselves everywhere and ended up resembling the dying sounds of some brightly colored birds. In short, it was a whole world that should have connected me with my roots, but I didn't know how to stay there . . . And then, also, there were those foreigners who behaved in Africa as in conquered countries, arrogant and odious.

"It is me whom the ancestor, sitting under the tree, has chosen to emigrate; he has designated me as though I were a soldier, as though I were born here, born to suffer and to emigrate. He told me softly, without insisting: 'It is you, Salim, who will succeed in saving the tribe, you and some others. There will come a time when they will follow you, and another time, you will follow them. You will walk without complaining, without ever whining, and you will cross the sea like an angel, like a beautiful and light bird. Go, Salim, the Spirit of the ancestors protects you.'

"I don't like thinking about the day I decided to leave, to follow my star. What I erased in a single stroke one night when the mercy of God and his Prophet mocked me. I have since then been reduced to nothing: a shadow wandering in the desert, where I have known the burning of hunger and thirst, these flames of hell. I walk, I run with other outcasts, my brothers, those like me, lost and dazed, but who have held on to their souls and their breath that keeps them standing. I follow the shadows that walk without turning around. Sometimes I pass them, and then it's my turn to look straight ahead.

"We arrived at the end of the desert one gray evening when I saw distant lights, houses, men and women, cars, flies, and birds of many colors. I saw horses and donkeys, lazy camels, young girls in light dresses. I saw or thought I saw a city bearing a strange name, Zagora. A flat city where people eat dates, are very kind, peaceful, humane. Adel, a very skinny guy, approached me and said, 'Come sleep at my place, the kids will be happy to have a guest.' I followed him and had some delicious dates. I was hungry, very hungry. I especially needed to wash myself, dive into a river, and get rid of the dirt collected after being on the road for so long. He accompanied me to the hammam, paid for me, and waited for me in a coffee shop next door; after an hour I came out a new person; he also gave me clean clothes. Adel worked in a hotel; I don't know what he did there, but I think he had a good position. I slept like an animal that had escaped the slaughterhouse. I had dreams, a lot of dreams. In the morning I woke up another man. Adel suggested finding me work, but I wanted to go to Tangier; it was an idée fixe. In Senegal, the country of my grandmother, they spoke of Tangier as the gateway to paradise, Tangier as the city where the two seas meet, door to Africa, window on Europe, the city where everything was possible, life, the crossing, death, too. They called Tangier the princess of seas and sands. Tangier, it's a city of all possibilities; from its coast you can see the Spanish and European lands. Tangier, the deliverance, Tangier, the Life . . . Yes, the hell, but also paradise . . . Adel felt that I was beginning to babble incoherently. Tangier had nothing to do with the misery and death that struck so many of my African brothers. When you are forced into exile, you get up and start walking, nothing more. It's very simple. No need for extensive analysis and studies to explain this action taken for survival. It is a pure desire to act, instead of staying put and praying to heaven, which, in any case, is indifferent. Have we ever seen anything coming down from the sky other than rain, snow, and some bits and pieces from a fallen star?

"Destiny is full of holes. Death must be in one of these holes. That's why it's better not to insist, not to go near to see. That's why I looked beyond toward the light that awaited me on the other side of the sea. I thanked Adel; we held hands for a long time, and he gave me a bag full of dates, water, and bread made by Fatma, his wife who had a tattooed chin. He told me: 'Here, we see Africans passing by, human beings born to suffer. But they don't stop, they continue their way as though they were running away. I know they are afraid of being rejected by Whites whose arrogance is equal only to their stupidity. I know how they feel. I've traveled through Morocco and I, too, was a victim of prejudice. My skin is not as black as yours; it's brown and it must scare them. I was born from a mixed marriage, and that is not always well tolerated.' I could have told him that I too was mixed, but he might not have believed me. It's hard to see. Black one hundred percent. And I don't want to abandon my role; I don't want another destiny.

"I joined my six companions, and, without telling them about my experience, I resumed our walk in silence. We stopped at an oasis where there were some goats and shepherds. One woman gave us some bread; another one offered some galettes* dipped in oil. There was a magnificent silence. Few words, few questions. These people are used to walkers going north. We left at dawn. A shepherd followed us and after a while turned back. Had he been trying to join us? In any case he was much too young to bear the journey and must have felt discouraged. Curiously, our appearance didn't frighten anyone. Perhaps these people felt toward us a kind of silent complicity that was obvious in their gestures of generosity, their smiles, and in the way they waved at us?

"We gave ourselves nicknames because we didn't have any documents on us. I am called the 'Sage' because of the ancestor who chose me to guide the group. The tallest of us, he must measure one meter ninety, is called the 'Ciel'; the one who's slightly shorter than him is called 'Nuage.' And then there is 'Boutête' because of his big head, 'Boussac' because of the bag from which he never separates, and 'Klata' because he resembles a rifle. And the last one is called 'Gibraltar' because he never stops talking about it. We like these nicknames; they give us the impression of being new, of having no past, of having the promise of a wonderful future even more radiant than in children's books. I surprised myself one time by forgetting my real first name. The most important thing is to get rid of everything, including one's name and history. We are 'without': without identity, without last name, without first name, without money, without ties, without family, without memory, at least officially. In Arabic, such people are called 'Bidoun.'* It seems that thousands of men and women who have lost their country, their land, are wandering around a little like us, are looking for any kind of work, without having anything on them, without nationality, without memory. This is the case, for example, of the Palestinians who entered Kuwait illegally in the 1970s and who can no longer get out from there. The state exploits these men by forcing them to do the most painful work and housing them several kilometers from the capital in camps where there is no hygiene or security. Among them are some pariahs, some misguided ones from other countries at war. They are the ones, the Bidouns, whose fate is that of slaves who don't exist for anyone. When one of them accidentally dies, people say, 'God has taken him back, and, in any case, he never existed.' I am a little less Bidoun than my companions, not because I come from Morocco, but because I still remember my name. I have not quite renounced my identity, and I walk holding my head high and thinking that this test will help me feel good about myself. This skin, I rub it, I mistreat it, I scratch it until it bleeds, I curse it; then I change my mind, and I start to love it and make it shine during the full moon. And then, I remember Nabou and her goodness, Karim and his love. As for my father, I feel sorry for him. He is not happy. He has not found his place in this world. Sometimes I feel responsible for him. This must be why my desire to emigrate is strong.

"A few days later we arrived in Ouarzazate. There is a city inside the city where they make films. Here one can easily meet a supporting actor, dressed as a gladiator, who is seen calling from a public phone booth while smoking a cigarette. Someone suggested that we work a few days in a historical film. But we would have to wait two or three days for the filming to begin. So we went to the mosque at the entrance of the city and asked for their hospitality. Someone who introduced himself as the imam asked us if we were clean. Yes, we were clean; we had washed in the oasis before entering the city. He insisted, 'Have you made your ablutions?' No, no ablutions. He then told us where the bathroom was and we made our ablutions. The imam didn't imagine for a moment that some of us were Christians or animists. Though I'm not a believer, I had to say the five prayers behind the imam, who took himself very seriously. After praying, I saw him talking energetically with someone. A few moments later, the young man to whom he was speaking arrived with round bread, butter, and honey. We didn't know how to thank this man who took us all for Muslims. Nuage wanted to say something, but Ciel silenced him by giving him a discreet pat on the back. Our religions had to be put aside. We weren't expecting so much hospitality from Moroccans. But then things got worse later on. The farther north we traveled, the less hospitable people became.

"When the day arrived, the guy from the movie came back and offered us five hundred dirhams to be part of a crowd screaming at a gladiator as he passed by. I asked that we be paid in advance. The guy said, 'Don't you trust me?' I said, 'No, I don't trust you!' For once, our black skin earned us some money. We were given costumes, shields, spears, and we were asked to stand for hours without moving. Was this filmmaking? Around noon, we were each given sandwiches and a bottle of soda, and we had to stand still all afternoon. If one day, at the movie theater, you watch an American movie filmed in the Ouarzazate studios, you may see a small group of Africans who look bored and are sweating under a ruthless sun. If you think they have survived, they may be sweeping your streets.

"Was it because of having spent the day in a setting where everything was fake, or was it because I was very bored while there that I had a funny dream that night? When I woke up, it all seemed so strange to me that I was convinced it was someone else's dream, a dream that chose the wrong sleeper.

"I don't know where I am, but I'm sitting in front of a beautiful young woman. Next to her is an old man pedaling to turn the wheel on which he's sharpening knives. I wonder why this man, so badly dressed, wrinkled and tired, has the favor of such a beautiful woman. I feel out of place. I try to remember where I had seen this lady. I stop trying and say to myself: Anyway, it's just a dream; soon you'll wake up and forget all this. Something holds me back, as if I'm stuck to the ground with something that smells like mothballs. Impossible to move, to get up, to change position. The lady has a very disturbing look, and I see again this advertisement where a man is hanging upside down, his feet glued to the ceiling. I have fallen into a trap. Suddenly, the woman takes a sharp knife, as if she is about to slaughter a lamb. The blade is shining. I see stars and try to stay awake in my dream. She tells me:

'You're a storyteller, so you'll tell me stories, beautiful and fantastic stories where everything ends well. I hate sadness and grief.'

"She doesn't give me time to say anything, tells me in her soft and sweet voice that if I don't fulfill my role, she will kill me:

'Tell me stories; if not, I will cut off your balls.'

"I immediately feel pain between my legs. Here I am in the role and skin of Shahrazad. I better not slip away or lose the thread of my storytelling. In spite of the woman's beauty, her black eyes express harshness, even cruelty. Tell stories to save my skin. But I have never been a storyteller. So I understand that I have to start writing if I don't want to die.

"I tell her, 'I'm neither a storyteller nor a writer. I have spent my life in the shadows. Now my life is in your hands.'

"She starts laughing loudly and suddenly disappears in a whirlwind caused by a sandstorm.

"I woke up with bitter saliva, my face tired and sweating. Nuage asked where I had spent the night, and I answered, 'At Haroun al-Rashid's*.' He thought it was a nightclub, because he was convinced that I had managed to go have fun with foreign movie extras. I didn't deny it. He laughed while repeating: 'How lucky, how lucky you are!'

"Our troubles began in Marrakech. There, we really scared people. They looked at us as if we had escaped from prison. Our overall look was certainly not very reassuring, but we are not criminals. We made the mistake of wanting to sit on the terrace of the café La Renaissance, a chic place in the city. A waiter immediately came to throw us out. 'You're going to make our chairs and tables dirty,' he dared to say to us. It is true that our clothes were not very clean and covered with dust. But refusing to serve us despite the money we placed on the table, it was unbearable. We couldn't lose our temper, as he could call the police. The waiter pointed us toward a hammam on the other side of the square. It was a good idea, except that he added this disgusting comment: 'Rub your skin well, and with a little luck it will be less black, less dirty!' The guardian at the hammam forced us to shake out our clothes before entering. He was right because there was a lot of sand. The hammam was empty, without any light. The guardian must have done it to save money and said to himself: I'm not going to switch the lights on for these Blacks. Klata suddenly screamed as if a viper had stung him. 'Don't worry, it's just a jinn,' I said, laughing. According to a legend, darkness favors the release of the jinns from their hideouts. After bathing, we went to a small brochette restaurant and then decided to buy some new clothes. It was important not to draw attention to ourselves. Klata was furious because he had pain from the bite, but we didn't take him seriously. He cursed in silence.

"I didn't know Marrakech, but I knew that in the medina, there was a flea market where secondhand clothes were sold at very low prices. So, we could have very cheap and almost new clothes worn by French or American bourgeois. On my blue shirt were embroidered the initials J. B. Ciel affirmed that it had to be James Bond's shirt. So I was immediately renamed 'James Bond.' I didn't have his size, age, profession, or physical and sexual prowess, but I liked to believe that I wore one of his many shirts. I said to myself: I'm no longer a Bidoun. I'm a J. B.

"We decided to divide into three groups and hitchhike, and we agreed to meet at the Casablanca bus station. The sun was in my eyes; I was sweating and was afraid of smelling of sweat. I remembered what my father once said to me: 'It had been my nightmare all my life, both at home and at school. One day, I had heard my father's first wife confidently say that Blacks have a strange smell, that they can wash themselves, but they stank anyway. She said: "As soon as a Negro or a Negress raises the arm, you are overcome by the smell of their perspiration. It stinks of urine. It's because of the nature of their skin, because the black color prevents the skin from breathing, and then everything comes out of the armpits." I was eventually convinced by this nonsense and thus was certain that I smelled as bad after the hammam as before. One day I even made holes in my shirtsleeves for my skin to breathe. I was crazy. Nabou was horrified by my reaction and told me that the white wife was so jealous that she didn't know what else to invent to make us leave. She then added with laughter, "Do you know what my father told me? He said that Whites smell of corpses! So, can you imagine? You'll smell of sweat, and your white brother of corpses! Stupidity is more common than intelligence, my son!" ' Remembering this story, I couldn't help but raise my arm and smell my armpit.

"The wait on the roadside was long and painful. The heat sent my blood coursing with such force that I was frightened. I took Nuage and Boutête with me. A truck stopped. The driver was not Moroccan. He was a Belgian who was returning to the port of Tangier, where he had to load some goods. At first, he said nothing, then, sounding like a cop, he asked us if we were from Congo.

'It's a shame, because the only Africans I like are the Congolese people.'

'But we have cousins in Congo; they are great, they work in Belgium.'

'Yes, but I want only Congolese in my truck, no one but the Congolese!'

"While he spoke, he slowed to a stop on the roadside and ordered us out of his truck; he had suddenly become enraged. He started throwing racist insults at us. This bad encounter made us think, and we decided to continue on foot. Boutête felt like crying. I gave him a friendly pat on the shoulder and we continued on our way.

"The walk between Marrakech and Casablanca was very hard, even if from time to time a truck slowed down more out of curiosity than generosity. My companions didn't speak, didn't sing, and walked silently, eyes fixed on the horizon. We slept in the forest, and we shared what there was to eat. Our money was hidden in leather belts, especially the dollars. Our savings of several years, years of deprivation due to this crazy and fixed idea, to leave, leave this dry land and go to the sea. Yes, the sea, we accepted it even though it was dangerous, and we took it straight into our stubborn dreams, into our nightmares. And how many times have I drowned? I screamed and no one came to my rescue. No sound came from my throat. One night I found myself alone in an inflatable boat that was slowly, irreparably deflating. All around me, the sea became a shiny mirror that reflected the moon, and I was abandoned to absolute solitude. My voice had been extinguished like the light that disappears beneath the horizon. I was emptied of all my strength. The inflatable boat was losing its form; I would sink when it completely deflated. I wasn't alone in having this recurring nightmare. It haunted our nights; we dreaded sleep. We were obsessed with crossing the Strait of Gibraltar. Sometimes I saw a swollen body floating on the water. Sometimes several bodies, children, women, some of whom were pregnant. I swam against the current, pushing aside with my arms these corpses that the sea sent us as a message to help us think. There was no need to think. We knew about all the risks and dangers, yet we insisted on this madness.

And I, grandson of M. Amir and Mme Nabou, son of Hassan the twin brother of Hussein, half brother of Karim, a Moroccan born in Tangier, I, the last offspring of a strange family, I was part of this journey and this nightmare. Impossible to go back, to revise the sheet of paper on which my destiny had traced a map and a route from the south to the north. We had to forget everything. I had put everything inside an old wooden chest, closed it with large padlocks whose keys had been thrown into the sea. This chest was sometimes made of wood, sometimes of iron. Sometimes it floated on the surface of the water, at other times it fell to the bottom of the sea and was taken over by enormous fish.

"I thought about my uncle Hussein and wondered if he had been happier than my father because of his skin color. He was a good businessman who liked money a lot. His cosmetics shops were always crowded. He was doing good business, and, before he got married, I knew that many women had offered themselves to him. He told me a little about his lovemaking in the back of the shop. I, modest and morose, didn't dare tell him about my little adventures. He considered that a young man like me could only have success with girls. When he asked me questions about my 'conquests,' I replied vaguely. One day, he insisted so much that I told him about my affair with our neighbors' maid. She was a discreet young woman with brown skin and long hair that the mistress forbade her to let down. She said Islam forbade it. One morning, she took advantage of her mistress's absence to go up to the rooftop and wash her beautiful hair while singing. I watched her. I found her very beautiful, attractive, and quite mysterious. I made a sign to her. She responded with laughter, then bent over and covered half of her body with her long hair. I had an orange, which I threw to her. She picked it up and bit into it as though she were kissing me. She sucked the juice and seemed to delight in it, as if she had never eaten fruit in her life. The next day, I threw her an apple. She polished it on her dress and kept it for later. We got used to watching each other from our rooftops. There was the playing with her hair, then belly dancing with the songs that were played on Radio Tangier, and then there was the first kiss when she finally invited me to join her. I took a ladder, placed it between the two rooftops, and found myself in her arms like an Indian movie hero. By the way, she loved the Bollywood productions that were shown at the Rif cinema in Grand Socco. One day when her mistress was away for a wedding in Casablanca, she invited me to join her in her mistress's bedroom. She was naked, lay flat on her stomach and told me she was a virgin. Without a word, I turned her over and we made love normally. She was not a virgin at all. Yet she swore with much force that she had never made love! Our relationship ended on the day her employers moved to Tétouan.

"Since I began walking, I have been thinking about Karim. I miss him. His tenderness, his affection, his big hugs, his words. If he were with me, he would show me the way, the good, the right. He had always been our light. I can imagine him smelling perfumes, classifying and commenting on them. I can hear him talking about marriage, recommending that I start a family, have children. I can imagine him becoming serious, his intuition telling him that finding the right person is difficult. Before dying, my grandfather had advised Ma to get Karim married. She had thought for a time to marry him to one of his nieces. Nabou was certain that the young woman would make him happy. Arranged marriage? Yes, why not, said Ma. But considering the difficulties involved in this project, she abandoned the idea and Karim remained unmarried.

"I also think back on the childhood memories that my father often shared with me. He still seemed very affected by the distance that had existed between him and his half brothers: 'When we were little, they ate at the main table with our father. My brother and I had to wait in the kitchen for them to finish, hoping for some leftovers. Nabou prepared us something else and fed us almost in secret. I used to be mad at my father, who didn't react to this. His weakness had always bothered us. A great gentleman, respected in his profession, loved by his two wives and his children, he could have been more courageous and not let us eat like the poor. Karim often joined us, sat down with us and made us laugh. It was his way of being supportive. Once he laid in front of us the tagine* that was destined for the white family. He had said, "Come on, let's eat together, and they'll eat our leftovers!" He laughed, and so did we. Batoule, the cook, was furious; she pulled away the tagine, rearranged it, and ran to put it on the master's table. Friday was the day when Batoule cooked two large dishes of couscous, one with meat, destined for the white family, the other without meat, for the beggars who used to come to eat at the doorstep of the house. One day my brother and I sat with the poor and were eating with them. When our father saw us, he became angry and ordered us to eat at his table. It was a small victory that Karim was proud of.'

"While on the road, only once, a bus stopped, and the driver signaled us to get on. We understood that he was not going to charge us. He said to me:

'Anyway, I don't have many customers; I will have you get off before our arrival in Casa so that my boss doesn't see you. He is nasty. He doesn't believe in God or his Prophet. He only believes in money; he is so rich that he doesn't even know how much he has, and he lives like a pauper. Tfou!' And he spat.

"He then asked if we were hungry. His assistant gave us some bread and olives. They were delicious. We were exhausted; this man had probably been sent to us by one of those stars that come to the aid of desperate people. He could guess we were going to try to cross the strait and gave us some advice:

'Be careful, the smugglers are your worst enemies. Don't trust them. Not at all. And don't trust Moroccans, not all of them, because some don't like us.'

"I stared at him and realized that he was métis.

"As decided, he let us down a little before Casa. The evening was beginning to fall. The lights came on one after another. There was a lot of traffic. We were on our guard because we knew that this city was not kind to the poor in general and toward people like us in particular. Casa is said to be the lung of Morocco. It is mostly an industrial city, with green and posh neighborhoods, and slums where people are violent among themselves and where life has little value. The poor are very poor and the rich are very rich. Casa scared us. We should not stay here long; we would never be safe here.

"Here we actually encountered the worst difficulties. From the bus station, where our little group met, we went to the port district looking for a cheap hostel or a small hotel. We needed to wash up and get some sleep. But each time we tried to enter one of these places, a guard chased us away, shouting at us to go back to our bush land. Once, a security guard got involved and blew his whistle, which brought a police van within a minute. Three policemen surrounded us, preventing us from moving forward. I was asked by my companions to explain our situation to them: 'We are just passing through,' I told them. 'We don't want to stay here. It's Europe that we want to reach. Be kind, let us continue our journey . . .'

"One of the policemen was black like us . . . Here was good proof that Moroccans can be black . . . But he was stupidly mean and called us 'Nègres,' 'Kahlouch,' 'Azzi*,' 'Abid*' . . . I didn't need to translate them to my companions, they understood: nigger, Negro, slave . . . Thanks to this policeman's superior, kinder than him, a white-skinned man, we escaped from being arrested. The security guard threw some insults at us, followed by remarks half in French, half in Arabic: 'This is all we needed! Kahlouchs in our country! The police are too kind to them. If it were up to me, everyone would be thrown into the sea, yes, the sea. They only need to swim up to Tarifa in Spain!'

"The black cop's behavior intrigued me. Why was he so mean, so ferociously racist, stubborn, and stupid? He too probably experienced racism from his colleagues or his superiors. He must be the son of a slave brought back from Africa. Wearing a uniform and carrying a weapon made him feel important. But he had to unleash his bitterness on those he arrested, White or Black. Maybe he hoped for a banknote or two? We knew it was the practice, but it was beyond our means. Nuage and Boutête, exasperated by what had just happened, in turn expressed their hatred toward Whites. Racism against racism. Black against White. White against Black. What a strange normality. It's difficult to fight this evil that is innate in every person. I would have liked to give a little lesson of good citizenship to my companions, but it was neither the place nor the moment. Fatigue and despair intensified. I looked at them; sometimes I felt sorry for all of us.

"The small hotel without stars that ended up accepting us was called L'Esperance. An old woman who smoked all the time ran it; she called herself 'Hajjah,' as they call people who have done the pilgrimage. But right away she confessed to us that she had never set foot in Mecca, that she was Jewish and that she resisted, after the Six-Day War in June 1967, the pressure of the Mossad agents who had tried to make her emigrate to Israel. After telling us her story, she put us in two large rooms, warning us about fleas. Her clients, she said, were not of high class.

"She then made a gesture indicating we must pay in advance, which we did right away. As I was the one who spoke most fluently, she took my hand and said: 'Come have a drink with me. I want to discuss something with you, do you mind? I'll give you a good price for the rooms.'

"I was falling asleep. I drank an alcohol-free beer and ate a chicken sandwich that she had prepared for me. She told me about her son whom the Mossad had stolen from her. She would never forget this incident. She hated Israel. Her life was here, in Casa, and not elsewhere. When I asked her if she had a husband, she took a long puff on her cigarette, looked away, and then said to me, 'My most beautiful love story is tragic. His name was Si Mohamed, a Muslim, and I converted to Islam to marry him. But his family didn't want to hear anything. Never can a Jewess, even converted, become part of us; never, cried his father. Evidently, my relatives reacted with the same violence: do you realize, to marry a Muslim, it's to betray our ancestors, it's to plant a dagger in the heart, one day or another they will kill us . . . Si Mohamed and I eloped. The police were on our heels, and they caught us. His father, enraged, had publicly disinherited him and banished him from his family. And my parents left with a group of Berber Jews; I didn't hear from them again. I cried, I suffered, I went crazy. I think I am crazy. Some time after this tragedy, Si Mohamed, without warning me, rose in the middle of the night, went to the place where his father had cursed him in public, and hanged himself on a hundred-year-old oak tree, dry and pitiless. I learned later that his mother had lost her mind and that his father prospered in his business. This happened a long time ago in the small town of Khemisset. A traditional town, a godforsaken place, with illiterate people . . . Nothing like Casa or Rabat.'

"Her eyes were wet. I wondered if her story was true or if she had made it up to make the time pass. As if she had heard the question I had just silently asked myself, she got up and came back with a photo album. Si Mohamed had a thin mustache and he looked like Clark Gable. In one picture, they were both in swimsuits, holding each other, happy, her hair drawing curls in the air. They were very beautiful. In another she posed, looking serious, like Ava Gardner when she was older. Today, the poor woman, her face was swollen with alcohol and sorrow. Her story was so moving that I believed it.

"In the morning she offered us a breakfast of doughnuts, crepes with honey, tea, and coffee. She gave us some tips about how to get to Tangier:

'Take the train; hitchhiking doesn't always work. You may come across some good people, but it's rare. Here, as everywhere else, people are not very nice to the poor, especially if they are black. The train is better; buy your tickets, be in order so that they don't ask for your papers. You have destroyed them, haven't you?'

"We didn't answer.

"The train left on time. In our compartment, a man passed his time eating. He offered to share his many sandwiches with us. He seemed anxious, and eating in such a compulsive way seemed to comfort him. From time to time he was burping, pronouncing just after each burp the phrase 'Hamdoulillah' (Thanks to Allah). When we arrived in Kenitra, he fell asleep. His snoring was louder than the sound of the train. A young woman, her hair covered by a pretty scarf, entered the compartment. She looked worried, as though she was running away from someone. A man, much older than her, rushed upon her and tried to force her to follow him. We didn't understand what he was saying, but his aggressiveness was that of a jealous man who wasn't very sure of himself. She tried to escape his grip and fell on me. I got up and helped her to her feet. There, the man gave me a look full of hatred and spat on the floor. He said in French: 'This is all we needed, niggers flirting with our women!'

"The ticket controller was a tall guy, friendly and smiling. When he took our tickets to punch them, he stared at me and said: 'You, it seems to me that I know you. Aren't you from Tangier?' I replied that he was mistaken, that I had never set foot in Tangier . . . The train arrived in Assilah, a small town on the sea. Armed police officers got on; they were searching for a fugitive. I heard that he was bearded and had explosives on him. All the train passengers were in turmoil. At one point, there was a lot of noise. The gendarmes had managed to catch and disarm the man. He was apparently getting ready to blow himself up at the Tangier train station. When the train started moving again, we felt relieved, but still worried. A passenger told us that the Moroccan police were impressively efficient, and they were able to dismantle any terrorist cells in formation. Thumbs down, he said to me: 'Al-Qaeda, nothing doing in Morocco . . .'

"We arrived in Tangier in the afternoon. I saw the couple that was fighting earlier. They were holding hands and kissing each other from time to time. It was weird. I gave up trying to understand these people. I had a strange feeling, as though I were discovering this city for the first time. Yet nothing had changed since my deportation. The Avenue of Spain was still crowded with families who bought ice cream at the Valenciana. The train station had been moved out of the city center, and it was turned into a police station. The harbor entrance was still being guarded. Ship ticket sellers ran behind immigrants' cars. Black women with babies in their arms were begging. Other beggars were chasing them away. I told myself that poverty made these miserable people very mean to each other. Racism everywhere, Whites against Blacks, Blacks against Whites. If these people had a lot of money, they would be nice to each other, compliment each other by having a drink together on the terrace of a big hotel. I observed all this with detachment. Here, I was at home, yet elsewhere. I was a stranger, and yet from here. It was a funny feeling. I had to fight against giving up everything and joining my family. I was tempted to let my companions down, but I had to go all the way. I was curious, and, at the same time, I feared the worst.

"The group was decided. Me, I had some doubt. I told them that before the crossing, we needed to think carefully, make inquiries, take all the necessary precautions, and especially not take all our money out at once. Since my return to Tangier, from black, I became white, a child of this old city where all kinds of scheming are possible. My trip from Dakar to Tangier was long and painful. Now I knew who I was. My skin, of course, had not changed on the way here. Neither my black skin nor my white mask. Racist, I had become at times, by hearing insults being thrown at me. I was so angry at these poor creatures who believed themselves to be superior because they were less dark than me.

"We managed to get an appointment with a certain Roubio; he was thus called because he had dyed his hair blond. He was going to put us in contact with an agent of Dib, the famous mafioso whose face nobody knew, who was as much a kif smuggler as an immigrant trafficker. We were told to wait for him at night in a café in Socco Chico. He would recognize us. His people informed him about everything.

"The Central Café was empty. It was late. From time to time the waiter came to ask us: 'Are you waiting for the boss? Be patient, he can be several hours late or not come at all. Patience, my friends!' In the street, the homeless were looking for a place to sleep. Children were fighting over a cigarette butt on the ground. An old woman was walking slowly. Two tourists were settling down on the terrace; a deadly thin guy quickly joined them. He asked them to follow him. The café waiter glanced at me to indicate that they were men who love boys. I didn't say anything. At night, Tangier found again its legends, its bandits, its lost souls, and its addicts. We were waiting for the man who would decide our fate. Tomorrow we could be either in Spain or in prison; or we could be at the bottom of the strait, where the waters meet, where the Mediterranean meets the Atlantic. We were all very tired. Our eyes were glassy. Our faces strained by this long journey. I saw three Africans passing by; they were well dressed and pressed ahead when they noticed us. Who were they? The waiter from the café informed us that they had just received their stay and work permits; they had been regularized along with thousands of others. He added: 'Morocco doesn't want to be seen as inhospitable. Many are given permits. That's the best thing that can happen to you if you decide to stay here. But don't talk to the boss; if he finds out what I told you, he'll fire me.'

"Around one o'clock in the morning, a big black Mercedes with tinted-glass windows finally stopped in front of the café. The street was for pedestrians, but some people allowed themselves to ignore it. A tall man got out, turned his head to the right and then to the left, spoke into a microphone hooked on the inside of his jacket, then signaled that everything was under control. A small man, short, his face wrinkled, appeared. The café boy rushed forward and kissed his hand. One of their men came to see us and asked for the password. 'L'Afriqueestmalpartie, Africagotofftoabadstart,' I said quickly.

"He slowly repeated, 'The A-fri-que-is-mal-par-tie. Af-ri-ca-go-t-off-to-a-ba-d-st-art.'

'Do you have the money?'

'We want to talk with Roubio.'

'Do you think Roubio will come here for so little?'

"Each of us took out his little hoard wrapped in several paper towels and handed it to the man who stood before us. He telephoned someone, and I heard the word 'weather' then 'East Wind.'

'The crossing will take place tonight; you're lucky that the weather is bad. The East Wind is strong. Normally this discourages the Guardia Civil. We used to do the crossing in good weather, which was a mistake because we were quickly spotted.'

"He counted the money, put it in an El Corte Inglés plastic bag, rushed back to the car, and started it very quickly. Then he backed it up, poked his head out of the window, and called the tallest among us, the one whom we had nicknamed Ciel. He spoke to him in the ear for a good minute, and then resumed driving at full speed, disappearing into the night in the medina, a perfect scene for film noir.

'So what is the message?'

'Appointment at three o'clock in the morning at the Merkala, at the far end of the blue point, east side of the lighthouse. Warned us to be careful, there are some nasty dogs. We will have to be very calm and quiet. A man will come for us and take us one by one. We will also have to be very patient,' he said.

"It was at that moment when I had the intuition that we would not be boarding any boat. It was all claptrap, a load of shit. It was clear from a distance. But I didn't say anything and went with them to the Merkala. The lighthouse guard refused to let us go through. Our tall guy kept repeating the password to him, but to no avail. The guard wanted money, but we didn't have any more. Someone tried to jump the gate, but two enraged dogs prevented it. We scraped the bottom of our pockets and slipped the guard some coins. He opened the gate, held back the dogs, and pointed at the blue point—in the night we couldn't see the colors—then the man disappeared, probably to sleep deeply.

"Heavy and absurd silence. Fear visible on all the faces. So much sacrifice, so long a path traveled for this moment, decisive, primordial, a serious moment in our lives. Soon we would find out: life, death, the end or simply betrayal. The blue point is where the Mediterranean meets the Atlantic.

"The time passed with a predatory slowness. The East Wind was swaying the trees. We didn't even feel the coolness of the air, so anxiously we were waiting. Someone saw shadows, another recognized an ancestor who came out of his grave and might have followed us from Senegal. I saw nothing but the sea. The East Wind made little white sheep on the surface that appeared and then disappeared. The light changed; it became clearer. Not a single boat on the horizon, nothing, nobody, not even a plastic mermaid or a wooden horse came to our aid. Only a few gusts of wind reminded us of our condition. And then the sun pierced brutally, as if to announce that the game was over. We looked at each other, lowered our heads, and left the lighthouse without saying a word. The guard opened the big gate silently, not daring to look us in the face. The dogs didn't move. Our defeat was intensely bitter. Ciel hid his face in his hands to cry. Nuage broke down by throwing stones from the top of the cliff. The others remained silent.

"We went back to the café. The waiters had changed. Nobody could tell us anything. Yet we had not dreamed it; we were here last night . . . A customer who understood our tragedy leaned toward us and said: 'Don't tire yourselves. The police are on Dib's trail, and as for Roubio, he is in prison in Almeria since this morning. It's best to forget about your money for the moment. I work with the police, I know about everything. We have instructions to fight against human traffickers. I can help you in the meantime.'

"My companions refused his help. No more confidence. They disappeared among the Friday crowd that was preparing to go to the mosque. Our group no longer existed; I was once again alone. I had no desire to go to pray, to claim justice from God for my misfortunes. It had been a long time since I understood that when the poor, the social rejects, and the courageous lost people asked for compassion and mercy from God, they received nothing. Worse, it's only the bastards, the thieves, the exploiters, the criminals, and the imposters who get rich and then go to wash off their sins in Mecca. It is the victory of hypocrisy over justice. I couldn't.

"After so long a walk, so many days of suffering, we had been stripped of everything in less time than it was possible to imagine! I sat there stunned, before my warm café crème, paid for with the last coins I had left, my eyesight blurred by the discovery of so much misfortune. The café served its regular customers in the morning. I decided not to move, not to speak, and not to scream. Everything had become black, the sky as well as the faces, the walls as well as the trees. My skin was reflected in everything that I saw.

"Black, absolutely black, my skin was black even under my feet, as if I had painted them with China ink. My palms, too. No more doubt now. I was totally black. What good was it to remember the white skin of my grandfather? Nobody would believe me, would take my story seriously if I told it. My black skin was my identity, double, triple, mixed, troubled, scarred, burned, and even infernal. My skin revealed the Negro in me; it recalled my ancestors who were deported from Gorée Island to the Americas. My skin, deprived of pores for breathing, and my soul painted in indelible black made me a free man, ready to defend this liberty by every means, to defend it, and to follow the path it would indicate to me.

"I sat there all day long, like a stone, a large stone, like a rock full of hatred and anger, inhabited by terrible dreams. Children stopped and looked at me as though I were a living statue. They went away laughing. From time to time, a waiter brought me another cup of café crème, offered by the café. Once he handed me a cigarette. I took it, chewed and spat it out. My saliva was yellow and bitter. My skin began changing its color, as if the sun, while passing over me, was washing me, making the blackness of my body disappear, which was also the blackness of my soul. A part of my life was going away. My body was changing, my head was spinning, my feet were moving by themselves, and I didn't know where I was or who I was. After a long moment of silence or intense noise, I don't remember which, a hand was placed on my arm and a voice said to me: 'Come, let's go home.'"

Chapter 8

All the time during Salim's journey, Hassan had struggled to try to track him down. There was, of course, the telegram sent from a post office in Dakar, but it had been more than a year since the family received it. Hassan went regularly to see a cop he knew a little and who seemed pretty sympathetic. He offered him a perfume for his wife and asked: "No news?" "Nothing to report yet," the cop answered. Apparently, the fate of a missing young Black didn't interest his superiors. One day after a few beers, to reassure him, the cop told him: "You know, the missing, it doesn't exist anymore today. In the past, yes, it was possible during the time that we call the 'Years of Lead.'* I had just started working in this profession and wasn't asking too many questions, but I knew troublesome people were disappearing and we never found them. But it's all over now! You can relax; your son must be partying somewhere in Ibiza or Marrakech! You'll see, one day he'll suddenly appear like a flower, so don't worry."

Despite everything the cop said, Hassan was afraid. Perhaps his son was the victim of an error. Someone may have put drugs in his pocket, or he was mistaken for someone else . . . He avoided discussing the subject with his mother, who, patient and wise, prayed every evening and waited for the return of her grandson. But he sometimes confided in Karim, who, with his smile and tenderness, calmed him by repeating: "Sa . . . Salim will come . . . am sure . . . he's okay."

The months passed without news of Salim. In the spring, the house had to be made ready for Ralph and Juan Carlos, who were coming back to celebrate their anniversary. They had asked Nabou fifteen days before so that everything could be perfect. As Hassan was depressed, it was Hussein who came to help his mother prepare for the reception. Among the young men who were there to set up, there was a black man named Alain Delon. He came from Mali and worked for an English antique dealer who had retired in Tangier. For some time now he had his papers in order. Hussein asked him questions, hiding his family's situation and Salim's worrisome fate.

"And racism?" Hussein asked him.

"Racism is first and foremost related to poverty. I avoid finding myself with Whites and especially asking them for anything. They are full of prejudices."

After a moment, Hussein asked him how the Englishman behaved with him. Alain Delon sighed and then said:

"I do what I must."

Hussein didn't insist on details. He understood that the man sometimes had to satisfy some embarrassing demands. One didn't talk about such things.

Hussein remembered the countless incidents he experienced with his brother. He always admired his calm, his patience, and his intelligence. Hassan never responded to racist insults and always refused to fight back; such attacks always stopped fast without ever getting worse. At the mosque, where he rarely went, no one lacked respect toward him. But his faith was not very strong, and he kept himself away from all that was religious.

Hussein and Hassan had nothing in common with their half brothers Mohamed and Aziz, who went to Cairo, one to study philosophy, the other to learn clay architecture according to the tradition of Hassan Fathy.* They had been diverted from their studies by the Muslim Brotherhood to become theologians in order to disseminate the pure and the hard ideology of Wahhabism, named after a Saudi Arabian of the eighteenth century who was obsessed by its virtue and the strict application of Islamic precepts. They let their beards grow, dyed them with henna, wore white *tchamirs*, which are like long djellabas, and went from house to house to spread their beliefs. People politely dismissed them by saying they did not need their advice to be good Muslims. Later they had tried with Hassan and Hussein, who listened without responding to their well-honed speech. Nabou had not intervened; she had left them to manage these brothers who claimed to solve all problems with religion. She said they must have been brainwashed. Karim reacted badly to their preaching. He had uttered only one word: "Violent." They had no weapons and were not threatening, but he felt the violence in their hearts, and he read on their faces something that scared him. After that, they probably went back to where they came from, perhaps to preach elsewhere, perhaps in Mauritania, where a brotherhood was formed and prepared in the same school of thought as theirs.

Nabou could guess the reason behind the long absence of her grandson. And when Salim, one morning, came to the door of the house, she knew where he came from and asked nothing. After having kissed his grandmother's hands and then her forehead, he began to cry in her arms like a little child who had run away. He suddenly realized the worries and anxieties he had caused his family. He could have given some news, sent a message, a letter, a postcard, to reassure them about his condition. Instead, he had sent a telegram, and then nothing for months and months, to the point that his family might have thought him dead. But the situation had overwhelmed him. From the moment he found himself in the police van and when no one took what he said seriously, the color of his skin had become his only identity, his only reason to exist.

The evening of his return, Salim, his father, Hassan, and Hussein and Karim, his two uncles, found themselves together in the hammam. Like Nabou, none of them asked any questions. They were happy to see each other, reunited, and determined to move forward. Thinner, with gaunt features, Salim reassured them about his health. He laughed and said, "I went for a walk; it seems like the best of all sports."

After a moment, Hussein said to him, "If you want to make it in life, you need a job." One of their cousins, the only son of Uncle Brahim, had wanted to hand over his business before taking his retirement. After the independence of Morocco and the reintegration of Tangier, Brahim had turned his exchange office into an insurance agency, which was still run by his son. Salim immediately accepted the offer; it was quiet work with a regular schedule, and he could resume his life at his own pace.

The first few weeks at the agency went without problems. Calm and poised, Salim was a model employee who had no reason to be criticized. He felt good and wanted to start taking pictures again. One morning he put on his new clothes, shaved his beard, and presented himself very early at the police station of the second arrondissement. He hoped to get back his camera that the police had confiscated.

There were a lot of people there. Cops in plainclothes could be recognized by their habit of talking on walkie-talkies from which a barely audible voice returned. Women, peasant women, sitting on a bench, were waiting, with a resigned air; no one really knew why. Young people were playing on their phones. Women picked up at night were dozing in a corner. A cop shouted for his tea; the boy had mistakenly served him a Spanish white coffee. So he shouted, "I hate coffee!" Salim didn't know with whom to speak. He approached a man in uniform. He had a higher rank. Salim asked if he could speak to him. The man answered: "No time; go see Zrirek, he can talk to you." Salim noticed he was pointing to a blue-eyed officer. He saw him from a distance, remembered his misfortunes, and said to himself: I really have no luck. This guy is going to be spiteful with me, it's certain he's going to be unreasonable. Salim introduced himself:

"Hello, my name is Salim Ben Hassan. I live with my grandmother, Nabou, who works for Mr. Ralph at the Casbah . . . I would like to recover my Canon camera that you . . ."

The officer looked at him and burst into a nervous laughter.

"What camera? Who is this Ralph? One of those faggots who leads an easy life up there?"

Salim tried to tell him about his arrest a year earlier with other Blacks . . .

"Oh yes, I see. You are the guy who takes pictures to sell to foreign newspapers and give a bad image of our country! A traitor indeed! If there were no human rights and all this bazaar of associations, I would put you in the cell right away, and no one would hear about you anymore! But you're lucky, today we cannot do our job as we see fit."

"Okay. So give my camera back, it's my livelihood; I'm a freelance journalist . . ."

"Free what?"

"I am independent; I am not attached to any newspaper!"

"So it's worse! You go to them all. Get out of here and don't come back . . ."

Salim understood that he should not insist. He left the place feeling depressed. The camera was expensive, and he had saved over a long time to buy it from the only Indian store owner who remained in Tangier; the store was on Rue de la Liberté, just before Socco Grande. He now felt convinced that he had no future in this country.

Around ten in the morning, Salim went to join his cousin at the agency. He was bored all day and spent his time watching the boats leave the port bound for Algeciras or Tarifa. From time to time, a boat sailed by at full speed. He imagined himself at its controls. His cousin came several times to get his attention. He had to draft insurance policies; customers were waiting, and he couldn't spend the day dreaming.

Month after month, Salim's anxiety began to get hold of him without his understanding why. Something was bothering him; he began doubting his identity again. The photos he took with his cellphone were not of good quality. He didn't publish them on his Facebook page as he had stayed away from the social networks. He absolutely wanted to get his Canon camera back. It became his obsession. He spoke to his father about it. One evening, when the police station was closing, Hassan entered and tried to rummage through an office. His police-friend caught him and said, "Have you gone crazy? Your son is back, so what are you looking for here?" Hassan told him about the camera. "That's beyond me," replied the cop. "You need to see someone more important." Hassan left with the deep impression of having failed. He would have very much liked to show his son that he was able to help him. So he went to see the Indian in Socco Grande to buy the same camera. Unfortunately, there were no more left.

That night, a voice or lightning came in his dream and made Salim sit up, as if someone had entered his room and ordered him to get up and take the road to Tétouan and then Ceuta. He had been dreaming of some young people, perhaps his African companions who waited for him. He often thought about them and wondered what had become of them. Sometimes he felt guilty for having abandoned them. Salim got up, barely washed his face, pulled on two pairs of gray cotton pants, a sweater, an old parka, rummaged through a drawer, and took the money. Without looking back he went down the slope of the Casbah at full speed until he reached the bus station, where he boarded a shared taxi going in the direction of Tétouan-M'diq-Ceuta.

It was raining. The wind's ferocity had redoubled. The trees were swaying in a big whirlwind. Salim didn't care. Bad weather didn't frighten him anymore. Huddled up on the back seat of the old Mercedes, he was pressed against a sleeping old man. The man was cold. Maybe he was dead. Salim began to think of his father. He felt ashamed. So much sadness in his father's eyes, a man who had not succeeded in anything in his life. Black skin is not an excuse, he told himself. The idea of avenging his father, whose defeat showed on his face, all over his body, gave Salim courage. Then he thought about his grandmother. She had the look of sad and unhappy days. He drove these images out of his mind, closed his eyes, and felt like crying. Out of the question. He was determined to try his luck far, far away. He thought of America. Inaccessible. Canada. Yes, why not. Vancouver. He repeated this name and then continued to watch the downpour that hid the road and the landscape. It's better this way, he thought. I'll travel into the mystery of this thick, icy mist. Nobody will come looking for me there. Then he thought of Cuba. Perhaps he would find his mother there? Nabou had told him one day the story of his birth. He was ready for any kind of adventure. But Europe was at his door. Ceuta is in Moroccan land, it's actually a Moroccan city occupied by Spain for five centuries. A piece of Europe in the heart of Morocco, in Africa. So this is where he would leave for Tarifa or Algeciras. The rest he left undecided.

The following morning, after waking up, Nabou shook Hassan awake. Something had happened. Salim had left the house at dawn. His bed was made, his things were tidy, but the sheep-leather backpack was missing. His identity papers were in the drawer of the small chest. Hassan understood at once that Salim had left to try a crossing to Spain. He collapsed. His son had been humiliated at the police station and had not overcome this terrible vexation. He was so rebellious, so fiery and so committed to his independence, his freedom. Hassan looked at the faraway Spanish coast, so clearly visible this morning: "Will he be happier there?"

Nabou confessed to him that she gave Salim a little money. He had claimed that a friend lent him a sum and that he absolutely had to give it back. Hassan understood that it was to pay the smuggler. He went out immediately to see his police-friend and ask him for help. He wasn't there and Hassan was told that he was away. Hassan returned home convinced that a tragedy was going to take place. Salim had certainly gone to Ceuta, Melilla being too far from Tangier. For some time, it was here, in Ceuta, that the illegal immigrants tried the crossing. Most were caught and driven back by either the Moroccan or the Spanish police. Hassan called Hussein to inform him. His brother reassured him, "Don't worry, Salim will not jump the border. He doesn't have the characteristics of a *harraga**; he must have a date with a pretty girl, that's all."

Hassan hung up and wondered: What are the characteristics of a *harraga*? Someone who burns his identity cards and tries to cross to Europe? Someone who had been humiliated in his own country? Who didn't find work and was harassed by the police? . . . At the end of the day, he took a sedative and fell asleep.

During that night, at the entry point of Ceuta, the Guardia Civil fired on a group of sub-Saharans who tried to force the security fence installed at the place of the passage; it was impossible to break through. An officer fired first in the air, which caused panic. Salim was in the first line of the group, clinging to the fence, but the violent rain and the squalls made him stagger. He was hit in the heart by the second round of the machine gun. Others were wounded, but most managed to escape. The police hastened to hide Salim's body in Ceuta's morgue, and orders were given to deny everything. After all, this man had no legal existence, no document of his identity, and no trace of belonging. Nobody would cross sub-Saharan Africa to claim the body of an "unknown migrant." That was, at least, the conviction of the Spanish police. But not that of the ones who managed to flee, who left for Tangier early in the morning and began talking to everybody, telling them how, that night, the border police had murdered a handsome and nice young man.

Hassan fainted when he heard people at a café talking about what happened. He immediately understood that it was his son. At about the same time, the morgue doctor, who had come earlier than usual, found in the back pocket of Salim's trousers a postcard written in advance and addressed to Mme Nabou, Maison Ralph and Juan Carlos, Casbah, Tangier, Morocco.

The phone number was found in the directory. He immediately called the family to inform them.

Karim knew something very serious had happened. He had dreamed of his nephew running on the surface of the ocean. He said to himself: He is not a prophet. I don't like this image. In the morning, he went to huddle in his mother Nabou's arms and cried in silence.

In the afternoon, Nabou, hard hit by this great misfortune, decided to re-unite all her children in Ralph and Juan Carlos's house. Hassan was falling apart. They had all decided to sleep there and surround Hassan with their love. It was the only time Hassan spoke about Salim's mother; he grieved not being able to inform her.

Fifteen days later, the police showed up at their house. An officer in civilian clothes asked Nabou to see Salim's father.

"We need to ask him a few questions. It's simply routine . . ."

Since he wasn't home, she gave them Hussein's store address where Has-san was working that day. His brother asked for his help as he was going to receive an important order; he couldn't check the delivery and manage the store alone.

The cops approached him without violence. It was a bit like when one suggests to someone to have coffee and chat about the state of the world. Hassan, although anxious, concluded that it would not be too bad. He knew the machinery of the police and their ways well. At one point he thought of his half brothers who had joined the Muslim Brotherhood. Maybe the police wanted information on them. Or on Salim? Then he suddenly re-membered the camera. But he was mistaken.

At the police station, the interrogation quickly took an absurd turn:

"Last name, first name, date and place of birth."

Why did they ask him all this? They knew perfectly well whom they had in front of them, since they had come to arrest him . . . Hassan decided not to make any effort. He answered: "I want to drink a coffee and read the newspaper." Distraught by his son's death, he couldn't care less about their questions. His mind was elsewhere, and, anyway, he considered that his fate was decided. He ended up answering them nonchalantly, sometimes in Ar-abic, sometimes in French, which irritated the police who made him repeat his answers over and over again. A chubby little cop, wearing an old brown suit, a gray shirt, and a dark tie, shouted into his ear:

"If you, a Black, are the son of a man named Amir, well then, I am per-haps the hidden son of the queen of England."

His tone was so rough that Hassan decided to say anything he liked.

"My mother is an Arab and my father is a horse!"

"Are you making fun of us?"

"Africa is in a bad way."

"You're acting crazy to fool us. We know this technique. You won't get away with it so easily. We have pictures where we see you in Hay Saddam, a dangerous suburb. Blacks surround you, and you look at ease. What were you doing with them? What were you telling them? I suppose you promised them the paradise in Almeria. You make them cross the strait, you exploit them, is that it? Do you not know that our parliament has passed laws against slavery and the exploitation of poor people?"

"No, I didn't know. I don't exploit anyone, nobody."

"That's what we'll find out."

Suddenly, in a firm tone, Hassan screamed:

"Give me back my son!"

"Your son, Salim? But you know very well what he was trying to do in Ceuta. It's unfortunate, but it's his own fault."

Hassan suddenly shut up, took out a handkerchief, and wiped his forehead and his eyes. Then he said softly:

"The hedgehog is a rose that pricks . . . the donkey and the ginger . . . the minaret has fallen and they hanged the barber . . . the bad breath of the hyena has contaminated the police . . ."

The officers looked at each other perplexed. They decided to leave him alone with his delirium. In the adjoining room they began to talk while they waited. Obviously, Blacks are weird people, said one of them. The one called the "Intellectual"—because he knew all the *Columbo* episodes by heart—walked into the room. In the series, though naive-looking, the lieutenant solves all the criminal puzzles. In his deep voice, the Intellectual asked why Africans were being harassed recently. The others replied: "The orders are the orders." He calmly said to them: "You know, Africa is the mother of humanity and the future for all of us." Stupid laughter and some loose words burst out of them.

The police officers' obvious ill will toward Hassan was exacerbated by the interethnic incidents that had taken place the week before among Africans, all of them illegal, and by the firm instructions that the police were given. The press pointed to the inefficient police who took too long to intervene and separate the hostile sides. People had been killed by knife wounds. It seemed that an order had been given to send these illegal immigrants back to their countries. Every man with black skin was, thus, a suspect, as well as all those who might help them; it was in this context that Hassan was interrogated. The photos found in his son's camera had been brought out of the archives. A cop handed him one with Hassan in it, hoping to intimidate him and make him crack:

"And this one, do you recognize him?"

"It's not me, it's the hairdresser who was hanged because of the minaret and the muezzin who had only one ball . . ."

Another officer arrived with an envelope full of photos that he spread out on the table. The police informants had taken them. Hassan was in all the pictures, sometimes with other Blacks, sometimes with Salim or alone sitting on the terrace of a café.

"Are you going to tell us what you were doing with these people? And why you were alone at the café? Whom were you waiting for? With whom did you have a meeting? What role did your son play in this human smuggling?"

Hassan didn't respond. He didn't speak anymore from that moment. The cop went out, infuriated. Hassan was alone now in his cell with all the pictures before him. On the table, then on the walls, he saw lizards, giant spiders, fleas as large as flies, a bat, and a twisted face, that of a jinn. These hallucinations amused him at first. He smiled as he let his saliva drip on his shirt. He urinated on himself and had the sensation of a hot liquid that burned him. He jumped, and then he had a fit of laughter. It smelled bad. Now I need to shit, he told himself, to shit until the stench becomes unbearable, because I must stink, I must drive these people out by my stink alone. Then he dozed off and fell from his chair. He struggled to get up, cursed all humans, gathered the strength to stand up, was ashamed of his condition, banged his head against the wall until it bled. Tears flowed down his cheeks. He didn't wipe them. He lay down on the ground, curled up into a shapeless form, hid his face with his folded arms, and didn't move. His body was transformed into a strange, inert thing, a pile of gray and black stones, covered with a dirty shroud. He had entered into himself and no longer cared about what was going on around him. He had become an object that could be dropped. It could be thrown into a pit or awakened, washed, and presented before a harsh and ruthless judge along with other innocents; it no longer mattered. After a while, he fell asleep, but he didn't dream, a sign that his life, his blood, his body were no longer present and that only his soul resisted in a corner and retained his humanity.

The Intellectual was sent to visit him. He was horrified by what he saw. Hassan was naked, his clothes were torn apart, the floor was smeared with urine and shit. Hassan didn't speak anymore when he tried to talk to him. The Intellectual called the commander-in-chief. He arrived shortly with the doctor on duty, covered his nose, and made a call on the phone.

The next day, Nabou and Hussein, who realized that Hassan was in custody, presented themselves at the central police station. They were asked for photos to show that Hassan was from their family. When they were brought in two hours later, the cop at the reception desk said:

"Ah, it's a Black! Sorry, but you've arrived too late. A plane was chartered last night, and one hundred and twenty-eight illegal immigrants are on their way to Senegal. Others will be regularized; their files are being studied. But he is not part of that group. You see, we take care of them case by case, we are humane."

Nabou was in tears, and she hid her face because she had always hated crying in public. Hussein began to protest:

"But you don't have the right, no right! It's wrong, and it's racism. We will immediately file a complaint and alert the national and international press. Yes, we will denounce you, make a scandal. And I don't think your chief will appreciate it. You don't respect anything, not even the grief of a father who has just lost his son!"

At that moment, the police chief, undoubtedly a very powerful man, arrived and seemed at least a little more responsible than the others. He was tall, slender, had a chiseled face, and he looked strangely like General Oufkir*. He held a yellow folder.

"Calm down, sir, he's not gone. He was transferred to the hospital, to Beni Makada . . ."

Hussein turned to his mother, who had dried her tears:

"Maman, they sent him to the madhouse. Beni Makada is not a hospital; it's a mental hospital."

"Indeed, we preferred to send him to a psychiatric hospital for some exams. He lost his mind during the interrogation. He made incoherent remarks, claimed that his mother was a donkey and his father a tree, he tore his clothes, and did on himself . . ."

"A horse," corrected the officer standing next to him.

"In short, he was out of his mind, and he talked nonsense. So, we preferred to have him examined and see if he was just pretending to make fun of us. He even claimed that his twin brother was white!"

Hussein cried out:

"But that's absolutely true. I'm his brother. Hassan is my twin."

The police chief looked at Hussein, astounded:

"We have never seen this, one black and the other white."

"It happens, sir," said Nabou calmly. "It is very rare, but it does happen. This does not mean that my son is insane."

It is at this moment that Karim arrived like a burst of light in this miserable, gray, and damp police station:

"Has . . . Hassan, my . . . my brother, where is Ha . . . Ha . . . Hassan?"

The superior officer said:

"But it's a crazy family, my word!"

Karim took his arm, something that was not done, but the officer didn't resist. Karim looked at him, smiling, then began to tell him the story of this crazy family. He mimed scenes, repeated words, swore on the Koran, spoke of a beautiful tree in Africa, of Gorée Island, and convinced this man with the hard and ruthless face until he smiled and even excused himself on behalf of his officers who had mistreated Hassan.

He spoke with someone on the telephone and was heard saying, "Yes, no, I don't know . . . Of course . . . Yes, yes . . . Good, I'll be waiting for you." Then he turned to Nabou and the boys:

"An ambulance will bring him back. It's a mistake, it happens, you know with all these undocumented Africans who don't speak our language; we are very embarrassed. We are completely overwhelmed, and we wait in vain for orders from Rabat. But your son, Karim, I know he cannot lie; it is immediately visible on his face that he is a bright light. But, forgive me, is Karim your son as well? He is white, in fact, very white . . ."

Nabou lowered her head and said:

"Yes, Karim, too, is my son, though I am not his mother. He is the light that illuminates our family. I wonder what I would have become without him."

Karim took Nabou in his arms and covered her with kisses.

The police chief wiped his forehead. Overwhelmed by so many strange things, he returned to his office. After closing the door, he could not help asking one of his officers: "Tell me, how can a black woman, very black, give birth to a child so white, as well as to black and white twins?"

The officer merely responded:

"It must be the will of Almighty God!"

"Look in a dictionary for a scientific explanation for it, you idiot, instead of invoking God whenever your ignorance reveals itself!"

Hassan arrived two hours later, looking lost, in dirty clothes and with empty eyes. He smelled bad. Neither his mother nor his brothers dared approach him. He was like a broken man, returned from a trip where he nearly lost his mind and maybe life. For him, being absent from his mind was the only way of responding to nonsense and cruelty. Madness is often manufactured, polished, prepared, set in motion by others. Even if it is an exaggeration to say that "madness is the others," the others often have something to do with it, much to do with it. Hassan carried his crime not only on his face, but also on his entire body. He was black, and he was punished for the disadvantage of being born so. However, this was neither a flaw nor an error. Quite simply, it was part of being human. It would be necessary one day to discover why skin color determines men's destinies, why it saves some while it sends others directly to hell.

The police chief awkwardly attempted to give them some final advice:

"Above all, don't go out without your papers. An error can quickly be made . . ."

Hassan stammered the word "hammam," then joined his mother with a hesitant step, took Karim and Hussein in his arms, and remained motionless for a long time.

Holding hands, they all left on foot and didn't look back.

* * *

The storyteller picked up his belongings, leaving behind the bowl filled with coins, took up his cane, and disappeared as the sun set on the hills of Fez.

abid   a term meaning "slave," often used as a racial slur against black Africans

adoul   notary; marriage registrar; religious official

Ashura   Muslim religious festival occurring on the tenth day of the month of Muharrama; it is a day of mourning in Shi'a Islam because of the martyrdom of Hussein, but in Morocco it is a joyful celebration of the dead.

azzi   a pejorative term referring to a black person in Moroccan Arabic (Darija)

Bidoun   short for "bidoon jinsiya" meaning "without nationality," usually refers to a stateless social group of 180,000 people who are noncitizens in Kuwait

bon vivant   a person who enjoys life

brevet   junior high school certificate

burnoose   a long, loose, hooded cloak worn by Arabs

djellaba   a long, loose garment with full sleeves and a hood, worn in North Africa

East Wind   One of the characteristics of the city of Tangier, where the Mediterranean and the Atlantic join and cause this famous East Wind. Legend says that if it appears on a Friday, it would stay in the city for three more Fridays. The wind irritates people, shakes things up, and makes going to the beach and fishing impossible.

fortieth day   the mourning period for a death is for up to forty days in Islam

gandoura   a long, loose tunic with or without sleeves, worn mainly in North Africa

galette   a buckwheat pancake

hammam   like a Turkish bath, in Morocco

haram   forbidden by Islamic law

Hassan and Hussein   traditional names for twin boys in Muslim culture; they were the names of the Prophet Mohammad's grandsons. The two names are

131

basically the same, Hussein being the diminutive form of Hassan, meaning "good" or "beautiful."

Haroun al-Rashid   a main figure in several of the stories in some of the oldest versions of *The Thousand and One Nights*; he was also a historical person, the fifth caliph of the Abbasid dynasty

harraga   one of the many North African migrants who illegally immigrate to Spain, Italy, and France in makeshift boats. It comes from an Arabic word that means "those who burn" (in this case their identification cards).

hôtel de passe   brothel

Kaaba   a stone building in the Great Mosque at Mecca that contains a sacred black stone and is the point toward which Muslims turn when praying

Kahlouch   a term for "Negro" or "slave" in Arabic, now considered pejorative; it is related to the word for "black" (*kaḥal*)

kif   cannabis, smoked to produce a drowsy state

kissaria   a covered shopping center with multiple small stores

massrya   a bachelor pad (room or flat)

medina   the old Arab or non-European part of a North African town

Mahdi   "the guided one," is an eschatological redeemer of Islam who, according to some Islamic traditions, will appear and rule before the Day of Judgment

Mellah   the walled Jewish quarter

métis   of mixed race, people of European and Indigenous ancestry. The use of the term is complex and contentious, and has different historical and contemporary meanings

Mouloud   a term used to refer to the observance of the birthday of the Islamic Prophet Muhammad

muezzin   a man who calls Muslims to prayer from the minaret of a mosque

nikah mut'ah   a temporary marriage

Peul   also called Fulani and Fula, a primarily Muslim people who make up one of the largest ethnic groups in the Sahel and West Africa

ras el hanout   a Moroccan spice mixture

rassoul   a traditional clay-based cosmetic applied like soap in the hammam to make the skin soft

Sacrifice of the Sheep   (in French, "la fête du mouton") a sacrifice that is part of the Eid el Kebir holiday, commemorating Ibrahim's willingness to sacrifice his son Ishmael at God's command

Sahel a semiarid region of Africa that lies south of the Sahara and extends eastward from Senegal to the Sudan

salamalecs a show of politeness, deference, or flattery that can be hypocritical, affected, or exaggerated

Shahada the Muslim profession of faith: "There is no god but Allah, and Muhammad is the messenger of Allah."

Sunna the body of established Islamic customs and beliefs

sura a chapter or section of the Koran

tagine a Maghrebi dish named after the earthenware pot in which it is cooked

taguia a small cap that resembles a kippah

tchamir a tunic

Terrrrbahh! The Arabic word *terbah* ("you will win") here is spelled the way the lottery ticket seller pronounces it, phonetically; he means "Come win money!"

tolbas Moroccan musicians who often perform religious chants

Tuareg Sahara Berber inhabitants

Université Al Quaraouiyine a university located in Fez; some scholars consider it the oldest university in the world

Years of Lead a period of social and political turmoil in Morocco that lasted from the late 1960s until the late 1980s